CARRY HER HOME

ALSO BY CAROLINE BOCK

LIE

BEFORE MY EYES

CARRY HER HOME

STORIES

by

Caroline Bock

Washington Writers' Publishing House
Washington, DC

SPECIAL THANKS TO:

Mark Blech for the original cover art and bird drawings,
Meg Reid for the cover design,
Barbara Shaw for the typesetting, and

Library of Congress Cataloging-in-Publication Data

Names: Bock, Caroline, author.
Carry her home : stories / by Caroline Bock.
Description: First U.S. edition. | Washington, DC : Washington Writers' Publishing House, October 2018.
Identifiers: LCCN 2018031234 | ISBN 9781941551165 (pbk.)
LC record available at https://lccn.loc.gov/2018031234

Printed in the United States of America

WASHINGTON WRITERS' PUBLISHING HOUSE
P. O. Box 15271
Washington, D.C. 20003
More information: www.washingtonwriters.org

IN MEMORY OF MY PARENTS:
Morris (Murray) Blech and Louise Blech (née Garofalo)

TABLE OF CONTENTS

Part I

Part II

Part III

Part IV

CODA

PART I

The Understanding

H e didn't have to say anything to wake me. I had already taken to not sleeping. He paced the length of the bed. He'd left twenty dollars for emergencies in his top dresser drawer. He had to go. I had to understand.

"I'll be back on Sunday or Monday, or soon."

"You'll be back soon," I repeated. "You have to go now."

I was twelve, his firstborn, the eldest of four. I shivered under the quilt. I could understand—but I was dumb, wide-eyed, knowing only that mothers and fathers leave even though they say they don't want to go.

O, Tomato

You were the seedlings Pop and I bought at the garden center each spring. You were the earth turned with hoe and rake. The new plants pressed gently into rows. Watered with the green snake of a hose. Staked as you grew into late spring. Your white flowers begot more white flowers, and we waited through May and June in anticipation. We shook our fists at the birds, though we loved the birds and would later in the summer let them have their share; the biblical gleanings for the widows and orphans were theirs too. O, Tomato, some of you were ugly, misshapen, outcasts, and others, a few, perfect in our hands, but we had no prejudice against any of you. Heavy-hung, blistering fulsome in the sun, you were cultivated by Pop and me. Our aim was to harvest you before you overripened, before you hit the earth, before the ants and slugs stormed into the crevices of your skins. You were beefsteak and cherry and heirloom before heirloom was a farmers market's term for old stock and higher prices. By early August, viperous stems and leaves and weeds overtook the garden, no matter our diligence. No scent but mud and sweat and tomato plant hung in the air. Some of you couldn't hold the beating sun and slit open. Some never made it from garden to plate and were feasts for the wily squirrels and raccoons. The abundance by mid-August. We froze you in plump sauces for the dinners of winter. We ran out of jars. We experimented with gazpacho and bruschetta, cold soup and chopped tomatoes. Yet you were never more coveted than when you were selected off the vines under the high weekend sun while callous crows spied us weighing you in our hands. We debated whether to slice you, sprinkle your centers with salt and basil and olive oil. Pop roared and scattered the crows. "Let's have those tomatoes now, Toots," he said to me. "Eat up." Seeds dribbled down our chins. You were ripe in our mouths, and it was like eating summer.

•

O, Tomato, I spot you red and ready now in another garden, marked sustainable and organic. This is not my garden but a community one. The memories imbued with heat and earth scents. My daughter shouts for me and reminds me that we are here for you. I quibble with my twelve-year-old over calling you a vegetable. In school, she learned that you are a fruit, and I acquiesce. Without Pop, I own no hoe or rake, no skill at turning the earth, no sense when to water or to stake, and have no bounty to share. I leave my yard fallow as in a Sabbath year, the seventh year of the seven-year agricultural cycle, though for me it has been my entire adult life. A long time ago, I left Pop's garden, and I ignored him every planting season for my busy, busy life. "Tomatoes," my daughter shouts. "Can I eat one now?" Without waiting for permission, she plucks one and pops it into her mouth. Seeds slide out of the corners of her tomato-red lips. Her cheeks are full of pulp, and she is a force of nature, this only daughter of mine. "This is the best tomato ever," she rejoices across everyone's garden. More judiciously, she selects another for her basket, and another. O, Tomato, beauteous of all summer vegetables or fruits, let me recall the days when I picked tomatoes beside Pop, and ate one or two directly from the vine at his direction in his garden under the sun, and I was young, and I was a child loved.

Bundt Cake Pans

"You can't miss it, Toots. Get off the parkway and make a left. No, a right," Pop says.

"Where will I be?" This isn't an existential question. You're asking for a street name.

"Where do you think you'll be?"

You're not looking for a geography lesson.

"The Bronx," Pop says. "You'll be in the South Bronx."

"You could have said that."

Pop wants you to drive to the South Bronx, one of the toughest neighborhoods in the city in 1979, and you've never driven into New York City. He wants you to do this because the doctors have told him he's dying, though he doesn't believe them. Rich men can afford to get sick, he tells you, not him.

One more problem: You don't have a driver's license, only a learner's permit. Pop's thought of this. "Your brother will go with you. He'll take my license."

Pop is forty-eight, your brother fifteen. You're sixteen-and-a-half, and you have already failed the driver's test once. Parallel parking.

"What am I picking up?"

He hesitates. Your mother's side used to run numbers, family lore now with your mother gone, but with enough truth that you instantly think of all the illegal things you could find at the end of this journey: drugs, contraband, stacks of counterfeit bills.

"Bundt cake pans," he says. "You're picking up our order of Bundt cake pans."

Pop wholesales cake pans along with regular pots and pans. All the rage, Bundt cakes, with chocolate or fruit fillings and drizzled glaze, need a special pan with a tower in the middle. Bundt cake pans are his top seller.

"You'll take the station wagon," he continues. "You'll drive south on the parkway until you get to that exit, and you'll go under the El."

The 'El' is the elevated subway. You've spent your life interpreting what Pop says, some of it prosaic, some poetic.

Pop eases up from his bed. His pillows are gray and yellowed, his breath raspy and stale. You stand over him, and he says, "If we don't pick up and ship out the orders for the Bundt cake pans, we can't pay the bills."

Suddenly it's 'we,' as if he is coming too. But you've made sure he's taken his pills, which make it difficult for him to stand. You feel like you should be doing more for him, but being a runner for Bundt cake pans in the South Bronx shouldn't be one of those things. He's spent the week bedridden, insisting you tell your younger brothers and sister that he has a bad cold. It's not the first time. And this 'we' is a royal 'we.' He's referring to his company, a one-man operation, as 'we,' and still you wonder if you have misplaced people you should care about in life.

"Nobody will bother you," he says. "There are good people there like there are good people anywhere."

"And bad people?"

He shrugs.

"I know you can do this or I wouldn't ask. You'll take the parkway, you'll make that right, and you'll go straight under the El, and there it'll be: the factory for the Bundt cakes pans." Pop states this with his old confidence.

"Why can't I miss it?"

He sizes you up.

"It's the only building still standing at the end of that block," he says. "Everything else is rubble, burned down, ashes and brick piles, so I'm telling you, if you're my daughter, you can't miss it."

On His Lips

I never heard Pop say "I love you" to anybody in his life, though he could have said those words in at least four—no, five languages.

French was his mother's favorite. Before the war, she lived for a while in Paris and whispered "*je t'aime*" to him when his father was around.

Russian was his father, a bear of a language for a bear of a man. "*Ya lyublyu tebya.*" Yiddish was the language his parents spoke to one another. "*Ikh libe ir.*" More arguments than endearments were had in Russian and Yiddish.

Korean was for the girls in Seoul during the war. Even years later, he claimed he could remember the taste of tongue-burning *kimchi* lifted from buried pots across his cold, bare chest to his lips. "*Na-neun dangsin-eul sarang haeyo.*"

English was his mother tongue. He could have said these words to someone—he liked to talk—but they were never said around me, never said to me, his eldest. "I love you."

Homemade Sauce

Your family never called it 'gravy' like some Italian families. But then Nana had all the pretensions of table lace and cloth napkins even on days that weren't Sundays.

You'd think it wouldn't matter to Pop if the sauce was homemade or not. He probably ate spaghetti with ketchup before he met your mother, if he ate pasta at all, as Nana liked to point out from her perch in your kitchen.

The sauce had to be prepared from cans of Italian tomatoes, after you sautéed four or five chopped cloves of garlic in Italian olive oil. Don't forget the sugar. "How much sugar, Nana?"

"Not too much." Nana clicked her big false teeth in her tight mouth, her eyes never leaving you. "Do you think that father of yours is made of money?"

You'd add about a teaspoon of sugar. At ten, it was hard to judge.

You'd sprinkle in oregano, and fresh basil, if you had it. Ground black pepper. Salt, but not too much.

You questioned the difference between salty and just right, and you were told that you should know.

"Something's wrong with you if you don't know," she said, taking a taste herself. She didn't trust you. You might have been named after her, you might have looked like her daughter, but you were too much like Pop: cerebral, obstinate. Your words, even at age ten, his, not hers. You always had to guess how much sugar, pepper, or salt and face her wrath if you were wrong.

By now the tomatoes would have a high viscosity, the flame on the gas checked and lowered, the garlic pungent.

"Stir slowly. Use the wooden spoon," she instructed.

The same long-handled, unbreakable spoon she struck you with on other days.

"Don't use the slotted spoon," she said, pinching where no one could see in winter. "You'll make a mess that way. Everyone will think you're a *gavone,* raised by wolves."

Or worse: you were the girl who splattered red sauce on the white stovetops.

Making Beds

Pop never listened to anybody who told him they knew better, not even when it seemed to be in his interest to do so. *No man raises four kids alone, not a man like you—no regular paycheck, nothing to your name. Give them up. To the state. To foster care. Come on now, you know this is the best thing for everyone, don't you?* But he didn't listen, not to his mother-in-law, not to any of the relatives who said they knew better. *The way you make your bed is the way you'll sleep in it, Toots.* That's what Pop always said when there was nothing else to say, when he was done arguing with anybody, even himself.

Piggyback Ride

On Friday nights, we'd cling to Pop's neck and hips and back, and he'd shout and buck and growl. He'd be stripped down to his white undershirt, plowing past the plaid chairs like a tank gunner—"no, a bombardier of a B52," he'd say, swerving us by our green and pink towel-splattered bathroom and down the hall. Later we learned that he could never be a tank gunner. Claustrophobia kept him from tanks and crawlspaces and elevators and bear hugs. He wasn't a man easily boxed in. He had no wife, and we had no mother at home, nobody to say stop, halt. He'd veer around the dining room table, knocking over chairs, his freckled skin fired up, his sweat viscid. Eventually he'd roar, jostling us off. Abandoned, we'd scramble back to his side, vociferous in our fear that we'd lose him too. But he took charge. Ordered that it was time to clean up the messes we had made—the overturned chairs, the scattered towels, the dust raised like ashes.

Louise's Kids

Apple trees lined the lot where we parked our station wagon at the Hudson River State Psychiatric Center in Poughkeepsie. Crows swarmed on their branches. A sour smell festered from too much fallen fruit. Pop said we'd pick a few apples before we left. Make an apple pie. But first we had to visit our mother.

She'd had an aneurysm. Was brain-damaged and paralyzed, except for one arm.

Here is how our Nana explained it to us: "It's all your father's fault. The stroke. The hospital. He should have known something was wrong from the beginning. From the very beginning, my daughter should never have married him. And now there's no money. No insurance. No nothing."

We crowded around our grandmother. She had wiry hair, a Roman nose, hooked, twice the size of any of our noses, always wore a red velvet hat, even inside our house. Nobody told us anything. When would Mommy be better? When would she come home?

"Your father is going to end up in Hell, in the fires of Hell." Her eyes bulged, watery, blinking into our eyes until we turned our sight to the kitchen's black-and-white linoleum. "Into the ovens."

We nodded at this knowledge. She was older than any of us thought we'd ever be.

"But you, children, are you praying for your mother? Praying every night? Praying there's a miracle? That she gets better soon and comes home to you and to me? Pray, and remember: You are Louise's kids."

We assured her that we were praying all the time.

At the Hudson River State Psychiatric Hospital, patients scuffled through the grand main lobby with its marble floors and glass doors. They followed us—and they were bloated or emaciated, some not looking much older than Caroline, who was twelve, and a tall, sturdy girl.

"They mean no harm," Pop said, rolling out our mother in her wheelchair from the elevator, which was as large as a giant's oven. We were waiting, slumped in the chairs near the entrance, the vinyl sticking to our hands, keeping us in place. It was hot, sweltering inside that lobby. Patients shuffled by, some begging for cigarettes. Pop had stopped smoking years before, and our mother wasn't allowed cigarettes. A few asked for change, and Pop gave until he ran out of quarters or dimes or patience and swatted them away with his Sunday *New York Times Magazine.* "Got to finish this crossword," he said, gnawing at his pen, squirming in his seat. "What's the word for a conical cut?"

Our mother attempted to ward off the other patients too. She waved her good arm over her matted hair. Cursed them, her tongue swollen, the words misshapen. We yanked and pushed her wheelchair into a corner and surrounded her.

"Frustum," Pop said, studying the newsprint in triumph and adding big, square, precise letters to small boxes. We didn't want him to finish the puzzle because when he did, we'd go. We'd leave her for another week. We'd set this routine these past few months, visiting most Sundays, at least once a month—and strange though it was, it was familiar and that was all we wanted: the familiar, the everyday, the sense that we were still a family.

"Time gone," he muttered. "Six letters." Pop could block us all out with a six-letter word starting with "e." Other times we wouldn't let him ignore us—we'd pick a fight with one another, call names: fat, ugly, stupid, stupid, stupid. But at the hospital, we let him work his crossword puzzle in peace.

In our corner, we performed songs we learned in school. The four of us, Louise's kids, took turns dancing with one another across the floors littered with cigarette butts and candy wrappers. We hopped in our sneakers, our versions of the hokey-pokey. Our mother put her good hand in and her good hand out, and we twirled her around. We made her laugh; it wasn't hard.

Caroline paired off with Matthew. Surprisingly graceful, he tried to lead, though Caroline soon took over. Our mother mumbled, "On the two," as if we knew what that meant. Our other brother whined that he was being left out, and Caroline stepped back and said that Matthew should dance with him. The boys were sun-streaked, lithe, loose-limbed copies of Pop.

Caroline danced on, swirling, the knots of auburn hair flung off her back. Faster and faster, her arms whirled out straight, something fierce and dazzling. The roaming patients retreated to other orange vinyl seats and followed our moves hungrily and desperately.

If it were warm enough outside, the patients would drag their way out of the lobby's glass doors. They would drape themselves along the marble steps like some concert was going on, like they were hanging out on a Sunday afternoon on what could have been a university campus surrounded by a wide expanse of grass, the Hudson River along the horizon, apple trees along the paths. Some held their heads in their hands and chanted their own incoherent string of words or rocked themselves back and forth. Some cried.

Inside, we danced around our mother, and Pop worked on his crossword puzzle.

"Elapse," Pop muttered at the puzzle. "Almost done."

We urged our mother to look at us. Not at the other patients. Not at Pop. Us. Only us.

We wheeled her chair forward and back. "That's what it's all about," we sang out.

We asked her if she was sad; we couldn't bear to think that she was sad too. But she pulled it out of herself, from a place that must have never forgotten that she was a mother, and smiled a brave smile. What we wanted was love, and this was what we got. We prayed, some, and this was what we got. But we were still her kids. Louise's kids. Weren't we?

Pop threw the magazine down on the chair next to him. "Finished," he said. He finally glanced over at our mother. "Do you know what day today is?" he asked her.

"Monday?" Her tongue lolled out of her mouth.

"No."

"Thursday?"

We whispered the answer in her ear. "Sunday," we said. "Sunday. Say 'Sunday.'"

She winked at us; we were sure of it. "Sunday?" she said, as if giving up a secret.

"What happened today, Louise?"

"Mass!" she said like she was winning. "Mass on Sundays."

"What happened today in history? Your history. Our history."

We didn't know the answer, and we wanted her to guess; we

yearned for her to know, to pull this out of herself from somewhere in her damaged brain, or we'd all be defeated.

Pop ran both hands through his hair as if he would tear it out if he could.

Our mother fingered the oversized, faded cotton housedress she had on, someone else's dress.

"You remember, Mommy, don't you?" we coaxed her.

"I do," she said to all of us.

"What did you have for lunch?" he asked, drilling her like the teacher he was.

"I don't remember."

"Where do we live?"

"Maspeth?"

"That's where you used to live." We laughed at her mistake, and she laughed again too.

"Did your mother visit yesterday?" asked Pop.

"Nana always visits on Saturday so she won't have to see Daddy, or us," explained Caroline, somehow liking that she knew things her mother didn't. "She says it's all Pop's fault that you're here."

Pop shook his head.

"How old am I?" asked Caroline. "How old?" We could have our own questions to bombard her with this Sunday. We had our own unknown histories.

Our mother stared off, haggard and hollow.

"Mommy! You have to know. How old am I?"

Our mother closed her eyes.

"Time for us to go, Louise," said Pop. "Say goodbye."

"Am I going home?" she asked. This question came from her

lips clearer than any other.

Pop didn't answer.

We held on to her good hand, to the gummy rims of her wheelchair. "I want to go home," she said.

"Soon, Louise." He patted his face with a frayed handkerchief and blew his nose. He was as gray as those shuffling around us.

We wanted to hold him too.

"Time to go," he said. Gripping the handles of her wheelchair, he slogged her across the lobby. Even though we knew the drill, we followed and shouted out, "Don't go. Don't leave us. Don't go. Mommy!"

"Who are they?" we heard her ask Pop. "Those children?"

"They're Louise's kids," he answered her.

Pop maneuvered the wheelchair inside the elevator, his back toward us, our mother facing away too, and the doors rattled closed.

"We are Louise's kids," we repeated to one another.

Around the lobby, as the light streamed through the glass, the other patients watched us, hung their heads, lit their cigarettes.

•

When he finally returned, we ran through the lobby, through the glass doors, down the marble steps, and toward the leafy, fly-buzzing trees. These weren't dwarf trees with low-hanging branches laden with fruit; these were giant trees. At the sight of us, the crows dispersed in a great black cloud. We hoisted ourselves up to the top branches. We reached for the apples like we were reaching for sky. We filled brown paper bags with apples. We forgot about our mother, for a while.

We'd eat apples in the station wagon on the way home, sour,

crunchy, hard-on-the teeth apples, until we had stomachaches. Later, Pop would make applesauce with raisins, some Sunday nights an apple pie for us, and we'd have apples in our lunch boxes for another week.

Carry Her Home

I rode on that oversized industrial elevator with Louise to the fifth floor. That silver metal box gripped around me like a vise.

My throat dried up. I broke out into a sweat. I concentrated on not screaming at the elevator closing in on me. The smell of my own skin sickened me. Louise moaned, as if forcing sounds or words down her throat. The box creaked upward. I wish I knew some prayers. I tightened my hands around the wheelchair handles so I wouldn't fall to the floor.

Louise moaned louder and I swung her around, said for her to quiet down, that we were nearly there, as if we were in a car instead of a transport, as if we were both going somewhere instead of me leaving her—"Stop it!" I yelled at her.

She groaned and whipped her good arm out of the chair, her glasses dribbling off her shrunken face to her lap. "Shut up! Shut the hell up!" I said, stooping over the wheelchair, not meeting her eyes, ashamed.

The elevator rattled and cranked up, shrieking, and dropped. If we crashed to the basement at that moment, I wouldn't blame anyone but myself.

Finally the elevator swayed to a stop, and the doors opened on the fifth floor. I pushed Louise's wheelchair forward like an old man with a great load. Moans echoed from the ward behind the nurses' stations. Moans trailed down the walls. The walls were breached with moans, buckling toward me.

No one was working the desk, which was splattered with charts and forms and prescription pads. A bulletin board was tacked with official notices about the importance of hand washing, state holidays, and the health risks of spitting in public spaces. I circled around so Louise could see me now, so I could loosen my muscles, so I could breathe. I fixed her glasses back on.

"Where's the nurse? Or an aide?" I said, as if she knew. I wanted to get out of there, to get off this floor, out of this hospital, and never come back. "I can't leave you here alone. I'm not a guy who can do this. I'm not that guy, whoever he is. I'm not him. I'm going to do something." I didn't know what. What swirled in my head was I had bills and more bills, from the mortgage to the hospitals and doctors. Her parents had made it very clear that they had no money to help. Prayers, they had to give, but the money had been gambled away.

"You know what?" I said to her. "We're going to survive this. We're going to find you another doctor. I can leave the kids with your mother and save money that way, can't I? Where is the goddamned nurse? Nurse!"

I had so much to explain to Louise. I thought we'd have our whole life for me to tell her my story.

Her lips, once soft, kiss-ready, kiss-sure, skidded to the side of her face. Her tongue was swollen from the medicines. I didn't know why she needed so many pills. I wanted her old lips. Her bare back. Her strong arms.

Next to me, she struggled with her words, agitating the sounds, drooling.

"I'm going to get you home," I said. "I'm going to find a way. Soon."

Down a hallway, metal crashed to the floor. A tray or, in another life, a bomb. I backed against the cold cement wall. I could hear the moans, but I had an insane thought: these walls would withstand the bombs. They were strong enough. The bombs could drop, and we would be okay.

As long as you can hear the whistle, it's not going to hit you. That's what we all said to one another on that mountain.

I couldn't leave Louise.

Big brown eyes canvassed mine from behind her cat's-eye glasses. They read me. Louise's eyes. The eyes I'd fallen hard for. They were emerging from the fog. Her medications must have been wearing off.

"Louise?" I asked.

"My head hurts, Murray."

"I'll find someone to help us."

"No." This was a firm no. She repeated it with even more resolution. Her lips hung open, the seams in them splitting.

Footsteps approached, a nurse or aide, and thudded down another hallway.

I had this insane thought: I'd hide us both. I'd find a place. We'd miss the round up. I scanned the hallway left and right. I smelled urine; the stink saturated the air, and especially from the wheelchair in front of me, I realized. From my wife, Louise of the generous hips and lavender scents. I listened for more footsteps, said her name, "Louise," and urged her to rise from that chair. "Get up. Get up, goddamn it." But she didn't; she couldn't.

"Think of them," she said.

"Who?"

"Our children. Don't we have children? I dream of them."

"Four. Downstairs."

She shrank into herself, faded, and slipped down into the well of the wheelchair.

"Nurse!" I shouted. Nurse!"

"In the morning," Louise continued, as if trying to read her own jumble of thoughts. "And at night. Kiss them." Her mouth, the cracked lips, puckered the air.

'I'm going to pick you up out of that chair."

"Too heavy," she said.

Was she laughing? Right now, I'd even take her laughing at me.

"Not for me, Louise. Not for this *shtarker* of a guy." I spun the wheelchair around and down the deserted hallway.

The smell of food crept out somewhere—boiled meat and vegetables and opened containers of spoiling milk. It must've been near dinnertime. I had to get the kids home; I had to get Louise home. We'd go to her bed in the ward, gather up the photographs I put at her bedside, find her medicine, and we'd go. We'd get out of here. I'd make it work. I started running, pushing her forward, her wheelchair forward.

"Sir? Sir, what are you doing?" someone called out from behind us. "Sir!"

I glanced back. I remembered him vaguely from my other visits, the evening aide on the ward. There was something misshapen about him. He had a bald dome too big for his body. The chest hair clumped at the V-neck of his stained blue uniform. The gold chains. The obsequious smile.

I sped up. Louise's head fell forward, her breaths shallow.

"Hear me, Louise. Open your eyes."

Her head hung down on her deflated chest.

The aide huffed toward us. "Stop now and step out of the way! Louise needs her medication. She's late for her medication. She needs to be fed. She needs my attention."

I skidded to a stop near the stairwell exit—I had nowhere I could go with her in the wheelchair. I bent my head next to hers. Her breaths were faint and stale. "Put your good arm around my neck," I said, reaching behind her back, pulling her toward me. "I know you're tired, but I'll carry you, Louise. I can do it. I'll carry you home."

Delusions

I circled the square of the roof. The blue spruces billowed. Those evergreens grew against the house, shedding needles into drains and squirrels into crawlspaces. Pop was always threatening to cut them all down, but he was loath to kill any living thing. There was always work to do on that house and Pop did it all himself: carpentry, plumbing, wiring, when he had the time. I peered over the blue spruces, their scents ruffling the air.

From the attic window, my younger brother and sister screeched, "Caroline," and begged for me to stand back from the gutter, which jutted off its bearings and was blowing loose, clanging against the side of the garage. Some days, I'd get them to follow me anywhere, but not today, out on the roof, with the wind, with Pop below.

"If I have to come up there, Toots," Pop warned, but then he was always saying, "If I have to tell you one more time" or "If I have to get up."

From the night before, after he and I cleaned up the kitchen from supper—hard-boiled eggs, farmer's cheese, a loaf of bread, still warm from the Portuguese bakery near his warehouse—he said I had to grow up, that I was almost ten and it was time to understand that my mother was never coming home, never going to recover, that it was a dream—no, worse, a delusion to think otherwise. No amount of prayers would change things. There were no miracles, not for us.

This morning, a Saturday in October, on the roof of our single-car garage, gusts squalled around me, a nor'easter forecasted, full of autumn leaves and downed trees. My brother lurched halfway out the window. I ordered him to stay put, to be good, to listen, to know that there weren't any miracles, not for us. Ahead of me, the tar split with the sky.

"No!" Pop screamed.

I spread my arms wide.

At Cranberry Lake

We wanted to stay in a hotel, or a motel. We had never spent a night in a hotel, or a motel. "Preferably one with a pool," we said, reasonably. "An indoor pool. We never swam inside anything."

"We're going camping on a lake," said Pop. "Cranberry Lake."

He bought us a used canvas tent big enough for the five of us in an Army-Navy store. The tent stank of damp and feet. Heavy flaps hung across the front as a doorway. We practiced putting the tent up once in the backyard; the sides sagged along the middle pole, depleted, out of breath or wherewithal. The tent was also missing a stake, and Pop fashioned one from a tree branch. He said it would do.

The sleeping bags were new and able to withstand temperatures of fifteen below. Pop never bought five new of anything, and we were stunned into silence.

"I didn't buy used sleeping bags because I don't want us all to get lice," he explained.

"Lice?"

"Bugs that make you want to scratch your skin off, but you won't get them because these are new."

We touched the sleeping bags to our faces.

"And we don't want to be cold," he added.

"Cold? It's July," said Caroline.

Even in summer, Pop slept with four or five blankets on his bed.

He had been on a mountain in Korea, in the war, and the cold was still in his bones. The lice must have been there too.

He circled the camping equipment, inspecting his purchases, and asked us for the tenth time, "Aren't we all looking forward to this trip?"

We would rather be going to a hotel with a pool, we said, but we will go camping. We wanted to trust him.

Before we left on our camping trip, Pop, wielding a pair of barber's scissors and an electric trimmer, sheared off Matthew's and Howie's hair into military crew cuts. A Band-Aid was slapped on Matthew's neck and another on Howie's ear, marking where each one had tried to squirm away and the trimmer slipped.

We laid the sleeping bags on the wood floor in Caroline's bedroom. The bags were baby blue and mummy shaped and long enough to cover our heads. "A sarcophagus," said Howie, wiggling into the interior, always wanting to be the cleverest one if he had to be the youngest. He lay very still and said, "Look at me, I'm dead."

Pop also purchased a Coleman stove, gleaming new, forest green and silver, with four sturdy burners lit by propane gas. "We'll build a fire at night. The stove will be there for coffee in the morning."

"We don't drink coffee."

"We'll have it for emergencies."

"What emergencies?" asked Caroline.

He looked like he wanted to tell us that there could be bears or mountain tigers in the woods. We knew all that—Caroline had informed us in hushed tones that we could be eaten alive in the woods. We all had to stay together. They wouldn't attack all of us.

"You should always be prepared," he said. "You leave in the

morning thinking it's going to be another ordinary day, a boring day. The sun is shining, the sky blue, and you get the extraordinary, the devastating, the last thing you ever think could happen to you. That's why I bought a Coleman stove."

We balled up the sleeping bags, silky, slippery shells, and stuffed them back into their nylon bags. We'd be warm, we reassured ourselves. We'd have fire.

In the dining room, Pop pulled out a map of New York and unfolded it across the table. He pointed to where we lived: New Rochelle, within the red and blue and yellow road-veins of New York City on the map. He smoothed his hand over the paper and pushed his glasses up—square, black, practical eyeglasses—and peered at the map, running his hands through his wild head of hair. We all studied the map, as if we could discern from the roads and byways what Pop truly meant. Our mother was in the Hudson River State Psychiatric Center. We found Poughkeepsie on that map. But we were going way beyond the hospital, all the way north. Up one of the blue veins to the far corners of New York—a top corner of the map with one road leading in and out.

Pop pointed to a break in the green: Cranberry Lake. "Here. A state park in the Adirondacks, the High Peaks, between the United States and Canada. You should know your country's borders. We will camp right on the lake," he continued. "Paradise for a week."

"What about bathrooms? There are bathrooms there, right?" Matthew asked.

"No," Pop replied. "Latrines."

We looked at one another, confused.

"Holes in the ground, kids. Like in the Army."

We searched the map.

"Don't worry," he said to us. "There's usually a door and a seat. What are all of you worried about? I'll be there."

"What about the bears?" asked Matthew.

"Just small brown bears."

"How will we survive in primitive conditions like this?" asked Caroline.

He lost his smile and was gazing beyond us. "How do any of us survive, Toots? You do because you must. That's what history tells us. We go on because we have no choice sometimes, but to go on even if you don't know the way. Don't stop— "

"Will there be toilet paper at this latrine?" asked Matthew.

"I don't know. We should pack a few rolls. Add that to the list, Toots."

"I'm going to ensure my own supply now," said Matthew, leaving the dining room table and the rest of us to figure out how to fold the map back up.

•

At the campsite next to the lake, the biggest lake we ever saw, a lake bounded by hills, by shores with scrub and rock outcroppings and swarms of black flies like dots and dashes in the air, Pop announced, "We're going to fish and swim." We had pitched our tent, facing the flaps to the ice-cold water. The middle of the tent sagged, but Pop assured that it would hold if there were rainstorms. We lined our sleeping bags next to one another except for Pop, who laid his across the front of the tent, as if his body would protect us from intruders, from bears, from creatures emerging from the dark, still lake.

Matthew had found the latrines down the dirt road and pronounced them unfit. "Not for humans," he said.

We were the only people on this side of the lake as far we could tell.

He returned to reading the *I Love NY* guidebook handed to us by the camp ranger. The ranger had studied the four of us, a tangle in the back seat, and said to our father, "Doing this without the wife? You're a better man than me. Good luck. Obey the rules. And stay safe."

We slumped on the rough wood of the picnic table bench, smelling sickly sweet of bug repellent, swatting at flies, watching him study the guidebook, not knowing what else to do in the middle of nowhere, until he said, "A guy like me should take on Mt. Marcy." He continued, quoting from the brochure, "Elevation of 5,343 feet, or 1,629 meters. It lies in the heart of the High Peaks." He shoved the brochure to the side. "Highest of the high, how about that? I don't know where it is from here, but it's out there."

•

The next morning, the flaps were flat down on our canvas tent, lowered against the brisk breeze from the vast expanse of lake, or so we thought. We had to get up, find clothes and sneakers, race down the dirt path to the latrine or pee in the lake, or woods. But nobody wanted to move out of the tent without Pop.

"If we peed in our sleeping bags," reasoned Howie, "maybe he'd take us home?"

"Don't you dare," said Caroline, since she was now responsible for all the laundry in the house. She couldn't imagine how much laundry there would be after this camping trip. She'd be doing laundry until she was an old lady.

We shouted, "Pop," from the safety of our sleeping bags. Maybe he had gone to the latrine. Maybe he was just beyond the bend. "Pop," we screamed out to the woods. We added, "Murray," and then "Murray Blech," as if he would answer to his full name quicker.

We poked our heads out of the tent. The trees were rustling with unseen birds or squirrels or raccoons or even bears. The mist was riding on the top of the lake. The black flies had fled, for now. The fine puffs of our breaths leaped in front of us.

We hovered behind Caroline as she sniffed the air and pronounced, "We should wear our sweatshirts," she said. "He'll be back soon."

We all shivered in the early morning light. The fog affixed to our skin, making it feel stripped and raw, and we squirmed, not wanting to make the trip to the latrine in case we missed his return. We didn't know how to light the Coleman stove or start a fire, and we couldn't find the safety matches anyway to try.

In reverse birth order, Howie peed at the edge of the woods. Judy sucked her thumb. Matthew swore he didn't have to pee, then dashed toward the woods and did too. Caroline crossed her legs and waited before shuffling down the path, her feet jammed into sneakers.

Caroline was gone such a long time that when she returned, the other three ran to her, saying they were hungry. She remembered there were apples in the car, but the car was gone too. She ordered them to get dressed. They would do what they had to do. Do what they must. She didn't know what that was, but they had to figure it out—

And then something tore through the woods, stomping, breaking branches, panting, and grunting. Pop. His long-sleeved flannel shirt was torn along the sleeve. Leaves and sticks crowned his hair like a wreath. His dungarees were gravelly with mud and dirt. He was gasping, grabbing his knees. We looked behind him and finding no one, not a bear in sight, the car down the road, we felt particularly annoyed.

"Where's that map from that ranger?" he said, ignoring us. "I found the top of a mountain—imagine a guy like me making it to the top of a High Peak — but got turned around coming down. Had to make my way through the underbrush into a narrow ravine. Had a moment when I thought I was back in the Army, back in the mountains, and I was lost. I wasn't coming back." He bent over and put his head between his knees.

"You climbed a mountain without us?" we cried.

He limped away from us. "I had to find out if I was the kind of guy who could make it up a mountain if he had to."

"What if you couldn't find your way back?" Caroline demanded.

"What if I didn't come back?" he said to her. "What would you do?"

Pop's face was bloodless and buckled with sweat. He blew on his hands, and when no one, not even Caroline, answered him, he said, "You all must be hungry. I know I am." He gathered up a fry pan, popped open the cooler, and brought forth eggs and bread. "How about you kids get washed, and I'll fire up our Coleman stove?" He adjusted a knob and waved a safety match to the burners. The stove flared up. The fry pan dampened the flames, taming them.

He made the wedges of French toast—stale *challah* dipped in eggs and milk, a swirl of vanilla and cinnamon, and then fried in butter, piece by piece, waiting until one was done before starting another. He served us one by one, calling us to him by name to receive our share.

We drowned the bread in maple syrup. We still didn't forgive him. We went off on our own, down around Cranberry Lake where we didn't find any cranberries, only pine trees and outcroppings of rocks good for climbing and clouds so near they looked like they were floating on the water. We spent all day trailing one another along the lake. We didn't get lost at all, unforgiving children that we were.

•

On the last night of our vacation, Pop said he wanted to watch the lightning storm across the lake. "But you kids should go to sleep. We have a long drive back home in the morning."

We'd go to sleep on our own terms, we said.

Rain pattered down, first in gentle drops and then in driving gusts off the water, slanting, drilling our tent, where we had escaped to, leaving him outside. If anyone dared to touch the canvas sides of the tent, rain fell inside on us all. Yet every time we turned, we bumped into the side of the tent. The raindrops were as big as our palms, smelling of ozone and tree bark. The sleeping bags got wet, our faces damp, as if we had been weeping.

Thunder banged down on us.

Pop screamed and, inside our sleeping bags, we thought he was the wind. He screamed again, like he was hurt. Caroline fumbled, opening the flap. Under the starless sky, on his knees, rocking back and forth, the rain and mud swelled up around him.

"Pop?" we said in small voices.

"Stay there," he said.

Slowly, he rose from the mud and stumbled back into the tent. He tied the flaps back closed. "Everybody sleep," he said.

Pop fumbled into his sleeping bag, back into the smell of pine and dank and dirt. The wind howled and worked to pick up that used Army tent and pitch it into the night. The sides of the tent snapped back and forth, the rains of the lake sheeted against the canvas, yet with him with us, our breaths slowed. We drifted, floating.

And he reared up. He stared straight ahead into the blackness and tensed, listening to the winds and rains whip, and crawled out of his sleeping bag once more. Finding the nubs of our heads in the blue cocoons, he kissed each one of us, and then slept too.

Jones Beach State Park

Pop approached the Atlantic Ocean gingerly, patting down his freckled arms with handfuls of briny, blue-gray water, letting the cold seep in, his broad back muscled tough like a turtle's shell. He wore green bathing trunks striped with palm trees down to his hairy knees. He wasn't by nature a cautious man. In fact, that day, the hottest of summer by far, he drove us, his two girls and two boys between the ages of four and eight, to Jones Beach. He let us loose with only a warning to stay clear of stinging jellyfish, deadly undertows, and killer sharks.

"If you're afraid, stay on the sand," he said, abandoning his ablutions and diving under a seawall of a wave. We couldn't figure out what he wanted us to do: follow him or not? The tide streamed through our toes, threatening to pull us in. We waited for him to resurface, and waited, every father looking like our father, until we were about to give up, go build sandcastles or dig holes, go eat the cheese sandwiches and peaches packed away for our beach picnic in white Styrofoam and ice, when he reemerged and called for us to join him. "The water is fine," he said.

We climbed on his back, and he carried us all out to sea.

Star Bright

Danny stole my bike, a battered, baby blue boy's ten-speed. Pop bought me a boy's bike because he believed they were better made. I didn't tell Danny that before he ran off with my bike, after he and two of his friends caught me on the deserted playground of his all-boys Catholic school. It took all three of them to hold me down so Danny could feel me up. When Pop and I walked the block to Danny's house, Pop knew only about the bike, and even then, it took me weeks to tell him that it was gone.

•

Danny's mother saw us coming and met us on their lawn. She must have come from playing tennis, her hair in a ponytail, her white short dress showing athletic arms and legs. She said straight at Pop, "Your daughter is the one out of control. Needs a mother, if you ask me."

•

Danny was still in his Catholic school uniform: starched white shirt, the tails out at the end of the day, and a striped blue and red tie askew at his neck. His shot of brown-black hair was cut tight on the sides and fell over his eyes. He must have visited the barber often to keep it regulation, unlike my brothers whose dirty blonde would grow all winter to their shoulders until Pop snatched them up and shaved their heads down to their skulls in the basement with his clipper and trimmer.

•

"Caroline's not so bad," Danny said to my surprise. His blue eyes weren't looking at his mother anymore but at my tee shirt. I wasn't wearing the white one because I knew it was see-through. We had always been roughly the same height, even though he was two years older. In the weeks since the end of the summer, since he had felt me up, his shoulders had widened out and hips slimmed down.

•

"Under no conditions do I want you playing anymore with this girl and—" His mother sucked in a tiny breath. Her ponytail bobbed, and my Pop was studying her up and down, not asking more about the whereabouts of my bike.

"Do you know where this girl's bicycle is, Daniel?" asked his mother.

"Do you really think my daughter's out of control?"

"Yes." Danny's mom arched her back and smoothed her hands down the straight line of her white tennis dress. "You need to buy her a brassiere, Murray. Tomorrow. And then you need to come back here, without her, and we'll have a drink together."

Pop, who never played tennis, blinked several times and pointed us toward home, averting his eyes from me, which wasn't unusual— he had stopped looking at me a long time ago.

"I don't want you out of the house after school anymore," he said, as he hurried down the block. "I want you home. You hear me?" His face was bright red, but I think it was more to do with Danny's mom than with me.

•

That night, Danny found me up in the public elementary school-yard playground, my old school. I may have been in seventh grade and having to take a bus to junior high every day, but most nights I was there. Over the summer, the visit to the all-boy's Catholic school playground was an aberration, an attempt to see if I became any different, anything other than the awkward, moody, insistently motherless kid, if the places I visited were different. But no, I'd be that kid until I died. And I liked the schoolyard. I liked to come here after dark without my younger brothers and sister, and would keep on coming no matter what Pop said.

•

Danny pushed my bike alongside him and dropped it in the grass before claiming the seat next to me. Without saying anything, he began to swing too. The metal creaked, a slice of moon hovered over the fields, and he in a polo shirt with a school insignia patched over his heart, and me in my white tee shirt and cutoffs and supermarket cheap sneakers stretching out my legs as long as possible, swung beside one another.

"Your mother thinks I'm out of control."

"I think she's screwing her doubles partner."

"Does your father know?"

He shrugged, working on keeping pace with me. "They're getting divorced."

I considered this—pushing out my chest and lungs and legs, an obscene number of stars all around, though I wasn't sure about stars, didn't know about constellations, didn't wish on them, didn't believe anybody who told me to wish on one.

He flew upward. "Star light, star bright," he rang out.

First star I see tonight. But I had already seen too many stars. I pumped harder.

"Would your mother sleep with my father?" I asked, as if I had been considering this as my wish.

"Probably."

•

After a few moments, and without warning, in midair, I leapt off the swing. He followed, rolling next to me, wet with sweat and dew, reaching for me, his hands stealing under my tee shirt. I swung over him, straddling him, pinning his wrists, letting him howl, letting him shout, "Stop," before I lowered myself and kissed him. I kissed him hard into the dying autumn grass, kissed him with purpose and intent. He relented and kissed me back. I pulled up my tee shirt and rained my breasts down on him like falling stars, like meteors, like they could grant our wishes.

String Theory

The blue and white bikini knotted at my neck. A string bikini, a hand-me-down from a cousin, and my only swimsuit that summer I was thirteen. When I dove off the low board, the one I trusted at Saxon Woods Swim Pool, my dive was perfect: head down, legs together, barely a splash into the blistering cold blue. I was unaware of what had been plundered from me until the lifeguard, slouching in his chair, sparked his whistle and particles accelerated across the fumes of chlorine, bounding off the concrete, and the border of green wood benches, which edged the pool instead of trees at Saxon Woods. Under the gravity of his watch, I plunged back down to retrieve the top of that string bikini. Near closing time, he fixed his whistle on me once more, motioned for me to get out, and I did. By then I had acquired a tide bound of my own matter and energy. A theoretical framework surrounded my breasts, and I dove off the high board and disappeared.

In a Sunset Orange

Charles roared into my seventeen-year old life in a used orange MG sports car. His family was from Trinidad, & he was co-captain of the tennis team. & I was editor of the literary magazine. I had too many younger siblings in my house for us to stay there. His mother didn't like me in her home. She trusted in the Holy Spirit as much as she believed that her only child would go on to great things, if he weren't with me, who trusted no one, who had no mother, who refused to be saved by anyone. I was something feral in my love of poetry & her long-legged son, something not to be brought into the house. We had the MG with its stick shift & clutch pedal & bucket seats. His body odor seeped into the well-worn upholstery like brewed tea, especially after tennis, when he came for me, his mother thinking that he was still at practice. Arthur Ashe was her standard-bearer for her son. My love had dreams too; we had dreams & they involved seeing the world in that car. We ended where we began, driving back to the high school with its twin lakes out front & parking in the back, in the teachers' lot until the moon rose. Our tender bodies laid low, the MG our exoskeleton of sunset orange. I've never driven in a car like that again. And Charles? He's nowhere to be found. An Internet search brings up only other men with his name. If he looked for me, he would find me in an instant. He would see all the places I've been, alone. Once I knocked on the door of his parents' home and the lace curtains fluttered. I knocked harder. Maybe it was nothing but the Holy Spirit that made those curtains go askew.

Blue Crabs

The rain just stopped for we don't know how long—it's Baton Rouge in June—and it's ninety degrees and ninety-nine percent humidity. The road out of the airport is flooded. I'm riding in Jack's new red pickup, all dressed up in wobbly high heels, having just arrived— later I'll switch to cutoffs and a tank top. A cooler of beer squats between us. He's already had one or two but doesn't offer me any. I'm nineteen and far from home.

"We'll wait, Caroline," Jack says, liking my name enough to linger on it.

He hasn't looked at me yet, really looked at me, and he turns crimson now, as if I'm going to blame him for the heat and rain. Fires torch and spike in the distance. At Christmastime, when I saw him last, bonfires were lit so Santa Claus—Papa Noel down here— could find his way along the Mississippi to the bayou. In the middle of summer, however, those fires only mean that the plants, like the one Jack works at as a newly minted chemical engineer, are running twenty-four hours. The smell of burning oil scrapes the night air.

Next to him, all six-feet-six of him in a baseball cap from the Cleveland Indians, his hometown, on this river of a road, I slink down in the seat, feeling small though I'm not what any mother would call delicate or petite.

"Can I take my shoes off?" I ask and flick them to the back when he doesn't answer right away. I always used to like how he was parsimonious with words, meticulous to the point of fussy with handwriting, and how, on the other side of things, his shoulders squared out in old-school sweatshirts like he was college-boy Atlas holding up the world.

The waters recede slightly, and around us, people are climbing out of their pickups or big cars, but mostly trucks, muddy, older trucks, with canvas bags slung over their shoulders. They're scooping up what's been upended from the high waters of Lake Pontchartrain. "Blue crabs," Jack explains. "I've seen the locals selling them along the road by the dozen." I don't have anything to add so I let the silence stay strange, let it scuttle between us, wishing for cool air, for one of his cheap beers, for daylight.

Some of the crabs are thrown off toward the kudzu and grasses, but most of the locals keep sticking them quick into the canvas. It's mainly men, wiry in jeans and long-sleeved checkered or striped shirts, who are stalking the crabs, which climb on top of one another, knowing they are in the wrong place as the waters back down. With bare hands, they pluck the crabs off the wet road into the steamy air, shove them clicking and crackling into their bags, which are passed along, jerking with so many live crabs, to the women and children in the trucks or cars. Except in the pickup closest to us— she's breastfeeding her baby while two toddlers sprawl across her lap and three more are open-mouthed and sleeping in the back seat. Her eyes are also half-closed, a slip of a smile forming on the expanse of her face, and I don't know what to make of it.

I always figure other women are born knowing about kids. Even Jack says he wants kids someday. But he's five years older than me, with his truck and his job at a chemical plant along the Mississippi, whose factories send up plumes whether it's Christmas or not. Other women know their mothers: the woman across the road probably has a mother worrying about her. Or the lady on the plane, with the double-strand pearls, who asked me in the kindest Southern drawl if I was visiting somebody special. I answered with "My boyfriend, who has a new red pickup."

After a long consideration of me, she said, "Bless your heart, you should be careful about men with new red pickups. They always have something to prove." I'm sure she had a mother who gave her insight on such things, as well as the pearls.

Next to me, Jack is still, gazing straight away, so I try to stay still. One man is done collecting crabs and raises his bag high over his head, the crabs poking from the inside, wild and wanting, as he tosses them into his pickup and takes off. I'm ready to go too, to get out of this pickup, to get on with this trip where I'm supposed to decide if I'll transfer colleges and come live with Jack. He'll pay the rent, for all the food. He paid for my plane ticket down here. I squirm. My summer dress is damp against my skin, as is my new bra and underwear, which I spent all of my tips from waitressing at the Fish 'n Fry last weekend on. The backs of my hands are blue-veined, my palms slick. "We could try them." I add after another moment of silence, "The blue crabs?"

I have never seen him eat fish, not once in the two years since we met at college back in upstate New York, not any kind of fish, not even fish sticks. "We could collect our own," I offer. "Gather them up in the moonlight?"

He looks at me as if I've suggested we go out and dance naked.

After a while, the remaining crabbers lope back into their vehicles and veer out onto the highway with a blaze of headlights on us, even the family with the half-dozen kids. Some of the crabs survive; the others will be boiled or fried alive, cracked open, sucked clean. I root for the survivors as Jack reaches for the back of my neck, and in one swift pull jerks my hips and legs and face toward him, kissing me hard, missing my lips at first, aiming for them again, and then again, saying my name until I hate my name. My arms and legs jab out. I struggle for him too, my hands like pincers, tearing at his short-sleeve work shirt.

"Now you take care, honey" was the last thing the lady on the plane said to me. I should admit that I'm not someone who takes advice kindly. Maybe it must do with never having a mother to offer me any, or maybe it just must do with being me.

Instead of the waters receding, the rains begin again, quick and furious, and the truck won't start. Jack doesn't want to leave. He just made the first monthly payment on the truck. Within a half hour, streetlights blow out, power outages blot the lights from the airport and along the river; even the flames from the plants are snuffed. Two or three crabs lash against the windshield—the water rose that fast—and claw their way back toward the deep waters, toward their own salvation.

PART II

On His Way to the Palladium Ballroom in Times Square

The calls from the peep shows to come in and see *girls, girls, girls* trail Murray through Times Square. He is tempted. He knows what he could do with certain women, but not these skinny, listless girls. Not today. What he wants is the curves and lips and smells that make him think that the race isn't over yet, that he still has time. He's freshly showered, his skin stinging from witch hazel and a close shave. He has shined his only pair of shoes. He aches to convince himself that he is part of all this, the tumult that drives people forward here. The outline of his lanky legs and bony shoulders, of his outsized hands and wrists, shines in the store windows. He is wearing his navy blue suit, his only suit. He can see above most people's heads and is aware that nobody is paying attention to him, nobody knows him.

He lives in a dank basement apartment in the Bronx and is invisible. Usually he plays basketball until all hours of the night, pickup games in the park across from his building, until he breaks a cold sweat inside the heat of his skin, and he can sleep without dreaming of family, food, or sex.

From every direction, cars hurl through the streets with horns and shouts. The smells rise—of exhaust, boiled hot dogs, perfume shimmering from two pretty girls, maybe one a prostitute. He leans toward her, and she tilts her sharp-edged chin and swears toward him, "Go to hell." He shrugs, as if contemplating this very thought, and she barks a laugh at the pale rising moon.

Murray keeps moving until he comes to the corner of 53rd and Broadway.

All around him: neon lights, store lights, streetlights, thousands of lights. This city is built on pushing time forward, extending the day into night, and he feels exposed, at risk, alone, always alone these days. The dusk, that in-between time, pulsates lights and sounds and strafes the pavement. *Run. Run.*

Tomorrow he promised to visit his parents in New Jersey, on their chicken farm. Why the hell did they move from the Bronx to a chicken farm? He had volunteered for the Army to get off the farm. He had run then. Since the Army, since the war in Korea, these are his nights: driving a cab when he can fill in, taking a class or two at NYU, thumping basketballs against backboards, into hoops, basketballs like shots in the dark. He jumps at a car horn blast. A column of traffic converges on Broadway. An ambulance and fire truck careen by.

If he visits his parents tomorrow, his mother will cook for him, send him back to the Bronx with roasted chicken. He is starving now but has to conserve what money he has for the dance.

And he can't wait until this traffic light flicks green, until he is given permission to go. He squeezes himself between a taxi and a city bus and weaves through the crowds up to the dance hall window, where he pays the early, discounted cover charge, and takes the stairs two at a time towards the smoke and the dark and the triumph of saxophone and horns into the Palladium Ballroom.

Louise at the Palladium Ballroom

The Palladium's dance floor sizzles with more guys than girls, and the guys all look good—every tall, short, fat, thin, gangly, square, boasting, sly, grinning, serious, sallow, gorgeous one of them.

The music razzes up my legs, up that cherry red spaghetti strap dress. The lights are dimmed and hazed, and the air kicks hot on my arms. I could use another drink to ease the beating of my pulse. I am pretending that I always wear red and even redder lipstick. I am making believe that I am not thirty-two and on my way to being the oldest living virgin in Maspeth, Queens, that I am the girl you will ask to dance.

The regulars know how to dance like they are never going to stop: Killer Joe Piro, Cuban Pete, Augie and Margo, Little Paulie and Lilon, Michael and Elita, Gene and Camilla. Everybody is dancing, and I am perched on the very edge of the floor, which throbs like it's alive. And I'm in high heels, dipping my bare shoulders to the beat, tapping the points of my shoes. My hips sway—this borrowed red dress swishes against couples holding one another for dear life.

By twenty or twenty-one at the latest, all my friends and cousins were married. Even my younger brothers are engaged—to girls who graduated high school last year. I tuck my cat's-eye glasses into my purse. The world blurs into dancers and smoke, white dancers into black and Puerto Rican, this being the Palladium Ballroom on a Saturday night.

At least this Saturday night, I am out of Maspeth, out of

Queens, away from the cemeteries, from the expressway and factories and chop shops. That corner of Queens is as much a mountain village as a New York City neighborhood—everyone knows one another, everyone is related by blood or marriage, the better off are New York City cops or firemen. My father hit the number and bought our house for cash during the Depression, the last time he won big.

On the stage, the first band winds up. Everyone claps and scatters. The dance floor rests. Two bands a night play the Palladium, a top name like Tito Puente or Machito and his hot Afro-Cubans, bookended by a band like this, Roland La Siere, razor-thin, wearing a slim tie and having a big mouth. He's thrown off his tuxedo jacket with kinetic energy, somehow fast and yet slow. Did you ever see Frank Sinatra without his jacket on?

I run my hand up and down my side, and Marlene, breaking free of her dance partner, grabs it. "Louise, darling. You look like Sophia Loren tonight."

"It's your dress."

"No, it's you," she whispers.

I know I'm not for the guy who likes the skinny-skinny or for the eighteen-year-old, but I was for someone tonight. If not, I'd shrivel into an old witch. I'd be found wandering the cemetery across from my house like Miss Nina, the priest's sister, hair uncombed, shoes undone, raking among the graves, feeding the dead breadcrumbs meant for the pigeons.

Next to me, in a peacock blue dress, another color I didn't even own, Marlene squeezes my hand. Her velvet black hair is pinned on the side of her head. Gold hoop earrings hang from delicate earlobes.

Men stroll the edge of the dance floor right in front of Marlene and me. I start checking them off: not the big fat one with the skinny tie that barely touches his heart; not the skinny one with the bad teeth, who smiles at me with twitchy lips. He isn't the one either; nor the one looking like he's wearing his dad's funeral suit, or the short one, swaggering and snorting like a B-movie gangster, or the one in the plaid jacket cracking his knuckles out of tune, or the bald, pale, nervous one with the balled-up handkerchief, who edges toward and past me, skidding over to Marlene. She says to him, "Be cool and keep moving."

I have never seen another girl ask a guy to dance except Marlene. And no, please, not the one doing a Xavier Cugat imitation with slicked-back hair, a slip of a mustache, a snap of his fingers. I adore the king of Latin music, though my heart is always with Frankie. The imitation did a few off-the-beat steps in front of me, his shoes looking rough and worn, and I let go a smile or I would have burst out laughing at him. Marlene does, a minty, fake laugh, and squeezes my hand harder. I grin at her, and I almost want her to ask me to dance. My mother's voice rat-tats in my head: "You're always smiling, Louise. You think life is one big joke? You're going to see how funny it is someday."

"Maybe I should go?" I say to Marlene, even though it's just ten o'clock.

"You're not going," she says. "The night's not over."

The main act starts its first number: Latin, drums, fast. Marlene is asked to dance. I focus on shoes. You can tell a lot about a man by his shoes. A pair rapped toward me. These aren't new shoes. But these shoes are well-tended. Someone took a lot of care and shined them with a soft brush, made sure they were polished all the way around, not just the front. The shoes stop near me, one of them tapping to the music, no problem keeping up, making the beats with a nervous energy. I tap too and survey the room. Bodies skim across the dance floor—girls in even shorter and tighter dresses than mine. Clouds of cigarette smoke float to the ceiling. More people flock to the wooden floor. Heels click. The dance floor shivers, along with the drum snares.

The shoes keep tapping. Italian men always wear their good shoes to the Palladium, often new, from Italy, handmade, leather. You are not Italian. You aren't Cuban or Puerto Rican either. They care about shoes too, like flashy shoes, some even two-toned, some pointy, made from alligators.

Tap. Tap. Tap.

What do I have to lose? I'm the girl nobody wanted to marry when she was nineteen or twenty. I was too tall, read too many books, ruined my eyes and had to wear eyeglasses, at least according to my mother. I own twice as many pairs of sensible shoes as I do high heels.

You shuffle, left and right. You're out of here, Mr. Shoes. You aren't staying. You shrug with your whole body. I step toward you. The air around us closes in, humid, sucked of light as the houselights dim even more. Bodies twitch and fling against one another, defying the song that urges going slow, going nice and easy.

We are almost the same height. Your suit is far from new. A striped tie frays at your neck. Your skin is ruddy, raw from a close shave. You have made an effort to tame your black curly hair. You study the dance floor intently, as if getting ready to pounce, and after a long moment I finally say, "How about you and me dance?"

"Did you know *mambo* means 'conversation with the gods'?" you ask without looking at me.

"That's not what I asked."

I tap my toes, off beat, and you notice enough to copy me, off beat. If you're one of them, a wise guy, a smart-aleck, like every agent in my office, I'm leaving.

"If you don't want to dance," I say, and he says nothing.

I go. I head over to the bar and order a Cuba Libre. If my mother were here, she wouldn't think that a Cuba Libre, rum and Coke and lime, is a nice girl's drink. I could argue with her that it was 1960, not 1929. Instead, the bartender smiles at me and pours. I've tried Cuban rum in the office, after work, when Ed, a senior agent, bought a bottle of Havana Club from Cuba and shared it with all. I wouldn't smoke Ed's cigars, but I drank Ed's rum just to show him I could.

I fling back the drink and lick my lips. How unlike the way a girl in a red spaghetti strap dress should act. As if wanting to absolve myself, I dab a cocktail napkin to my lips, smear my red lipstick, stick the napkin in my clutch and fix, slowly, my lipstick until the bartender winks at me and says, "Looking good."

The band lets go another song. The regulars: Killer Joe Piro… Cuban Pete… Augie and Margo… Little Paulie and Lilon…. Michael and Elita… Gene and Camilla… The dance floor is packed with seven, eight hundred people and at this hour, a line probably snaked around the block, everybody wanting in. The walls vibrate, the building shakes, and the music rains, but nobody cares about getting wet. A purple haze lingers over the dance floor, a hundred cigarettes are being lit up, and I catch a whiff of marijuana; there's often that sweet smell in the club by now.

You step between the dance floor and me. "Am I a guy with bad luck? Is that why you walked off?"

"Am I a girl with good luck? Is that why you followed me?" The rum, at first so sweet, burns my throat. I sing off-key to the music, as if I can't help it: "Hey, mambo, mambo Italiano—"

"Maybe you should dance, not sing?"

"I am a much better dancer."

"So am I."

Your shoes might have been shined, but your white shirt needs a good ironing. You lead the way onto the dance floor. You concentrate, your head down, listening to the beat. It's the longest beat in the whole world. Everything seizes up in me, my heart, my breath. Maybe you are one of those awkward-step-on-your-toes-bump-into-other-couples-excuse-me-excuse-me kind of guys who never really learned to dance but only clump and clunk with the girl and apologize afterwards.

"On the two," you say. The dance is suspended between us. I count to myself. Dancing on the two means starting on the second beat, not the first, letting the first run through you, letting it go, leaving it in the air between you and your partner, dancing on the two. A suspension of time is counting on two. It's anticipation; it's having our hands and backs firm, our hearts ready.

You count one-two with the bones of your shoulders slightly rising. You take my hand, which is large, with square nails, which spend most of their days typing and filing and taking dictation in a government office. *And a one and a,* I say in my head. My high heels follow yours, a light step, sure, precise. You hit the beat. You dance, and even more than that, you mambo. I throw my head back and mouth, "Hey, goomba, shake it, shake it, shake it."

I grin but you don't. You move your hips only slightly like even with your talk of gods this isn't your kind of dance. "Don't you smile? It doesn't cost."

"I'm not a guy who smiles much."

I laugh, not because I'm the kind of girl who laughs easily, but because I want to see you laugh, want to let you know this isn't going to be the only dance. You concentrate. Your fingers direct my hips, pulling them close, then away, step left, step right, swing, back, turn, close, fingers on the small of my back, step left, step right, swing, back, turn, close. A sliver of a nervous tongue swipes across your full top lip. Your fingers lick around my hips, and somehow I sense you don't like skinny-skinny girls. You dance me into the crowded sea of arms and legs. Strong arms pull me in when the song ends. I have the urge to kiss your full lips right then.

The band takes a breather, takes the whistles and cheers with bouncy bows.

"Next dance too?" I ask.

You clamp your mouth shut as if your breath can be stolen, your face crimson. I've always loved men who blush.

"I like tall girls," you say seriously.

I stand at attention. "Tall girls with heels?"

You glance down at my feet. I turn my shoes in and out like I am Judy Garland in the ruby slippers, except I want to go anywhere but home.

By the ladies' powder room, a blur waves at me. Marlene. I can't quite make out if she was saying hello or goodbye. On stage, the band leader sips a short glass of clear liquid while the drummer twirls his sticks and the saxophonist blows smoke. The bandleader grabs the microphone. I know he's famous, but I like the less famous Roland La Siere more.

Your eyes rise from my shoes. "On the two?"

This is a slow dance, and you hold me as if I'll fall away.

In the shadows, you say your name: "Murray. Murray Blech." You hit the last two letters, hard and throaty, as a German would, and I wonder to myself if you know it means 'metal.'

"Louise Garofalo," I say, and wait, the longest beat.

"Louise Garofalo." You repeat my name thoughtfully, and it hangs in the air between us. I get it: you're not Italian.

"What's a guy like me supposed to think about that?" you ask, but it's not really a question for me.

"He's supposed to think that if he dances with me, he'll live forever," I answer.

You widen the space between us; smoke and darkness and music fill it in. "I'm not sure I want to live forever. In fact, I'm sure I don't." I sway my hips. "I'm a tall girl in a red dress in high heels. You like me." I step toward you.

And we dance, on the two.

We dance until three. The Palladium stays open until four in the morning, but the band always wraps up around three. Roland La Siere and his band are back on stage, and they are playing the last song, "Save the Last Dance for Me," a recent top forty hit by the Drifters. I am singing with them in my head. And as if you know I have the song in me, you hold me tighter.

The whole room sighs into one another, three or four hundred couples, our heat rising against one another, not needing light or air, only the sound of Roland La Siere and his band. If I only have tonight, I'm going to dance.

At that moment, lights flood the place. Women scream as if caught in the act of doing something other than dancing.

"Raid," shouts a cop and then repeats it in corrupted Spanish, replacing the refrain, where we should have whispered to one another, "Save the last dance for me." Police in full gear block the front and back exits. A few run for the doors anyway with a stampeding of high heels.

"Nobody leave," says the loudspeaker in English and Spanish again.

You look like you are going to run. "Stop," I say, not letting you pull away. "Come with me."

The police are grabbing apart black and Puerto Rican dancers from the white girls. They are raiding the back rooms and the bathrooms, searching for marijuana, cocaine, heroin. The cops surround the band members, who are protesting that their instruments are being indiscriminately handled. The saxophonist is shoved to the ground; the drummer's sticks are snapped in two. Roland La Siere puts his jacket back on and swears up and down the stage.

"A guy like me doesn't like to stay around and answer questions," you say to me. Your face goes hard.

I yank out my work ID, my official United States Army Division of Strategic Services identification card, from inside my clutch. Nobody is arresting Louise Garofalo, or her guy. I push it toward one of the New York City police officers blocking the main entrance.

He sticks his face next to mine and snatches my identification car. His breath is full of onions. "Don't look like you, sweetheart."

I pull my eyeglasses out of my clutch.

The cop leers at me. "US Army, really?"

"Yes, sir."

"Yeah? You look better without the glasses."

I snatch my identification card from his hands. "He's with me," I say, claiming you as my own.

"Yeah?" says the cop, eyeing you. "Get out of here."

We flee down the stairs. It looks like there's a party happening on Broadway. I press myself into your side. You step back on the sidewalk, glancing uptown and then downtown toward Times Square.

Out on the street, with my glasses on, your suit looks even more tired and sad. The shoulders droop, and your shoes—I can see now that the heels need to be replaced.

"Where do you live?" I ask.

"Where do you?"

"Maspeth."

You look confused, and I explain, "Queens. Right over the 59th Street Bridge. You can't get there from here at this time of night. You can only get there by bus, and there aren't many buses running at this time of night. A shame, isn't it, Murray?"

Distracted by the flashing police lights, the din, the hecklers and whistlers and shouters and sharpies, you mumble something, and it doesn't sound like English.

"Murray?" I say, holding on to your arm as the crowd suddenly surges off the sidewalk into the street, into the middle of Broadway, and is surrounded by more police cars and wagons. "Where do you live?"

"The Bronx. Across from Crotona Park. I got to get going."

"Wait." I wave to Marlene in the middle of a crowd flowing into the street, taking over Broadway like a parade or a march, and she is pointing toward downtown.

"I thought you had left," I shout to her.

Marlene is breathless. "I found some friends to hang with in the very private back room." Her dress is off her shoulders. Her voice, high-pitched, seems to dissolve into the sirens and squeals. "So, Ho-Jo's?" she asks. "We are starving. And the night's not over." She hurries on, a blue flash zigzagging down Broadway.

I turn to Murray. "Twenty-eight flavors, Murray? Of ice cream. Howard Johnson's? Open twenty-four hours?"

You shake your head. Say again that you should go, that you have to run.

You are looking guilty or trapped, and I wonder if there is something more here that I should be afraid of, or is it me?

You lunge through the crowd, across Broadway. I trail you until we are out of the theater district.

Mid-block, you stop and wait for me. "You can't get home from here, Louise."

"Sure I can."

"Go back to your friend. To the twenty-eight flavors."

"I can always find my way home." I am at your side once more.

"Lucky."

We walk until we are at the West Side Highway. The stench of the river seeps through the streets. A rat or cat darts from under a car and back under another. You scan the deserted pavement, the foggy streetlights, looking like you can't decide where you want to go, or if you truly have anywhere to go. Stubble plucks at your cheeks; your lips are dry and cracked, your sweat heavy and musty. I want you to kiss me. I've wanted it all night, and I'm tired of waiting. I go to kiss you.

You do a careful dance, as if you don't see me edging my face near yours. You raise your arm high. A yellow cab screeches next to us. "You should get home," you say, and open the door to the cab for me. Inside, the cabbie is a creature of the night: ghost gray, with odd lumps for a face and stomach.

I place my hand one more time on your shoulder. Your body tenses. You want me to get in the cab and go, so you can also go, and I ask you something that I have never asked any other guy, that is going to cause me grief with my mother. "Come to Sunday dinner?" I ask. "Tomorrow, or later today, actually. One o'clock."

"No. I'm not your type of guy, or the type of guy who gets asked to Sunday dinner. And your parents—"

I scribble out my address on the cocktail napkin in my clutch and push it into your suit pocket. "Please, come."

The cabbie leans on the horn, and you say to him, "Cut it. You have to wake the whole block?"

I ease into the taxi and you shut the door after me.

The cabbie, settling into his seat, pounds his horn again and tears up the highway. His bloodshot eyes seek mine in the rearview mirror. "I can show up for Sunday dinner, babe. 'Cause I wouldn't count on that guy."

I spin around, hoping you'll be there, acknowledging my impulsive invite. Yet as soon as the cab is on its way, so are you—the lone man hurrying down the street at four in the morning.

•

The dance floor would open up the following Friday with a posted sign that read 'Raided Premises' and a cop checking over people at the door. Within a year, the Palladium would be raided again and stripped of its liquor license. Marlene, however, would declare that the Palladium Ballroom was over. When Marlene said something was over, it was done with, finished, yesterday's news, written off, and after that night, the Palladium Ballroom was over.

The Day after the Dance

I should never have danced with her. Or I should have left her after that first dance, or after she told me her name. I should have left her after the whole night was over, after the cops busted into that second-floor dance joint. What was I thinking? I should never have held her so close that her perfume was all I could smell. Her scent was more like the ocean than land, something you sense before you see it.

But I've got to admit, she was good-looking in the way I like good-looking. That red spaghetti strap dress. Those strong arms keeping the beat. Tall, plus high heels. I like girls who aren't afraid of heights.

I could have asked any one of the single girls to dance that night. I was the kind of guy that girls noticed—for the six-foot height, for the square jaw and dimples like some artist's impressions—and then dismissed after a dance or two. I was also the guy with one suit, which hung off my shoulders like it was somebody else's, which it was at one point. I got to the Palladium early. If you entered before six o'clock, admission cost only fifty cents; it was two bucks after eight. I had one pair of shoes I was always shining up to look presentable.

I should have kept it to one dance with Louise. I should have left her after I heard her name, Louise Garofalo, and run out of there. Every Jew and Italian from Brooklyn or the Bronx or Queens, and plenty of others too, were at the Palladium Ballroom last night, and I don't know why she picked me—because truth be told, she asked me to dance, and I didn't say no when I should have.

She swept her arms around my own as if to steady me on the dance floor, her back straight, her shoulders at attention, and the strap of her red dress slipping off—and my fingers catching it, almost righting it, squiggling it back up her rounded shoulders, the warm skin, the sticking heat in my fingers, all of it distracting me. With the slightest of moves, a twist, a curve, an exhale, she pressed her cool cheek against my own. And she held on, clear-eyed and smiling that brash smile that made me want to ask her, "What's so funny?" But I wasn't the kind of guy who could ever ask a girl that, because what if she was laughing at me?

I needed something—a job, a girl, a future—but I didn't need her. Statuesque, marble-skinned, Italian, a Roman Catholic, from a neighborhood somewhere in Queens, she was not the girl for me.

She had on that red, red lipstick, and her lips broke open to a wide smile of straight white teeth. I should have run out of there. Instead, her lips to my ear, her pelvis to mine, her scent on me, lavender, a feral weed, our fingers intertwined.

Yet when I told her my name, I said it with defiance, wanting to scare her off. "Murray," I said, and she whispered back, "Murray." I was "Murray," a son of a Jersey chicken farmer, living in the basement of my father's cousin's building in the Bronx.

"Murray." She hummed, off-key, not letting me release her, leading as much as following. I could see she wasn't young either.

"Murray." She said my name into the air, and we danced, again and again, and she was in my arms when the band played the closing song, and in the middle of it all, the police raided the place. We were thrown out onto Broadway, into the crowd that somehow seemed to be having a good time out of it all. Get ice cream at three in the morning. Twenty-eight flavors.

I had girls before—girls I felt awkward with. A girl in Korea—I had encircled her waist with my hands; she was a sliver, half-starved, a girl-child, muted afraid or threatened, trembling under me. I should have let her be at that whorehouse. But I came back for more. I was desperate in that bitter cold to prove that I was alive. I had two girls at the same time on a dare from one of my Army buddies, who also took two at the brothel. I kept rearranging my two, head to toe and then both on me at once. I was drunk, and my stomach burned from the liquor and the *kimchi* dug up from their cold earth. I would never be a saint, but after Korea I vowed to myself that I would never pay another poor girl for sex.

I've got to admit, if Louise had known what I was like, she would have left me first. She would have thanked me for the dance—even if that first time we danced like we knew each other. But if she knew what I was, she would have left me on the dance floor or the street.

Before she left me, I should have kissed her.

Before she got in that cab, before she sped away and left me with her address and phone number on this damn cocktail napkin, her lips were near mine. I could have done it—gotten a taste of her—and been okay, been able to walk right out of there and onto the subway, back up to my hole in the Bronx with the memory of the kiss. I wanted to kiss her as much as I ever wanted to kiss any girl. Maybe if I had, it would have ended then.

Or I should have run.

But the cabbie honked, and I knew enough to hold the door open as she wrote down her name and address and phone number. I didn't have a telephone.

I leaned in toward her, thinking I'd kiss her fast then, but she was faster than me, lithe, slipping right into that taxi like how I imagined movie stars glided into limousines. The cab drove off, and I was there on the curb, thirsty, stomach turning, wanting nothing more than a kiss. I was also thinking that the cabbie was lucky. He got a good fare.

I've got to admit, I wasn't planning to show up for Sunday dinner today.

I had promised my parents that maybe I'd go see them in Jersey. How many times did I call them from the pay phone on the corner and tell them that? I was a *putz*. A *schmuck*.

Back in the Bronx, the streetlights were dim or blown out, the night starless. Not a body on the street. I felt like the invisible man— I was supposed to be reading, took it out of the university library, *The Invisible Man,* and I thought about how I got what that writer was saying. No one saw me either—though he had it worse, being a black man—but I understood what he meant when he wrote, "I am invisible, understand, simply because people refuse to see me." Nobody saw me at that dance at the Palladium, except Louise.

•

When I arrived home, my apartment was dark as a trench. Not a scrap of food in the fridge except a bottle of milk, which I gulped down, then wiped my chin and swayed as if I could fall asleep standing up. Cats or rats scurried up and down the three cracked steps that led to the door and across the street into the undulating shadows of the park.

I put that cocktail napkin with the lipstick smear and the address on the dresser next to me, and I could smell her in that two-room apartment. I yanked my mother's goose-feather comforter over me. My legs were at the edge of the bed, my feet cold paddles, and I wished I was outside with the night air—and the sense of possibility the moon and the stars always brought to my dreams. I curled into myself, alone as I'd ever been alone, thinking about red lips, about long legs drawing you into warm waters, about the fact that you couldn't get to Maspeth from here.

•

This morning, I got up and shaved. I slapped down my hair so it wasn't so wild, wishing I had time or money for the barber. All the while I was insisting to myself that I was only curious. I'd eat a good Italian meal. I wouldn't stay for long.

I wore my suit as I had the night before, but my other tie. I scrubbed my nails. Two trains and a bus plus a fast-paced walk through a neighborhood that had the German Sports League office in a two-story building on the corner, and me thinking, *Come on out, and I'll play you a game of Bronx ball.* I got so worked up I had to loosen my tie.

All this travel got me to her high, narrow brick house, to the Virgin Mary out on its square patch of lawn, marble, moss-covered at the base, to a field of cemeteries practically at her front door, and to the new cars, a black Pontiac GTO and a gold Chevrolet Impala, parked like they owned the winding wedge of street dividing the living from the dead.

•

And I pace across from Louise's two-story brick house. I should go back to the Bronx, find some guys, and get a pickup game going before it's dark. I am empty-handed. I should have found a bakery and bought a cake or some cookies. But all I have is a buck and a half and a subway token on me.

"*Schmuck*. You can't stay," I say out loud to myself. "You've got to go."

At 1:00 p.m. exactly, her father sits down at the dining room table. I can see right into their dining room through the open lace curtains. I may be in the gutter across the street, wearing out my shoes, but these streets are starved for space. I can see and hear them like I was there.

"He's not coming, He got what he wanted out of you last night, that's what."

What did I get?

"Maybe he got lost, Ma," says Louise. She enters the dining room carrying bread. The loaves are the length of her arms, studded with sesame seeds, cradled in a wood tray, an offering. As she sets the bread down, one loaf topples over to the white linen, and she rearranges it, brushing the seeds into the palm of her hand.

"Nobody buys the cow if the milk is for free, Louise."

"Ma, nobody's selling and nobody's buying."

"Your father," says the mother, clattering in behind Louise, "he likes to eat promptly, very promptly, at 1:00 p.m., Louise. We are starting our meal with or without your friend. And if you're saying and doing all this to shock me, you should know that I don't shock so easy." The mother states all this without even acknowledging the father at the table.

One thing I can't help noticing: this mother has a wonder of a nose. A nose dominates her face, commands, hooks over her lips and dwarfs her eyes. A nose sinks her cheeks, which are streaked with broken capillaries. To be accurate, it is a fine example of a Roman nose.

Louise stomps around her in a black skirt and pale pink top, and she is polished, professional, a bit chunky and severe even, something other than how I remember her from the night before. She wears a touch of pink lipstick and cat's-eye glasses and her hair pinned back. She looks like she is in disguise, like the woman in the red dress with the squint will swoop out from the wings.

"Let's eat," says the father.

"We'll eat as soon we're ready to eat," replies her mother.

"I'm sure he'll be here any minute," says Louise.

"We eat when I say we're ready to eat, Carolina."

"Do we? Are you cooking the meal, or am I? Where are your sons?"

The aroma of meat wafts out to the street. I imagine that I can smell the meat cooking and simmering from every one of these houses in Maspeth. The whole world here is sitting down to Sunday dinner. I feel like I can just fill myself up with vapors of other people's food. I don't have to go in.

Two young guys make their way to the dining room table with its white lace covering and matching plates and slink down in the plastic-covered seats across from the roast. They are of medium height with great heads of coiffed hair, which they slick back with combs that appear and disappear from their back pockets. They are snapping at one another, lighting cigarettes, being yelled at by the mother not to smoke at the table and doing it anyway with a pulling back and a shooting of the smoke at the ceiling. I don't have any cigarettes on me. Since the Army, I rarely smoke; smokes cost money. My shoes, dusty and gritty from the long walk, look even worse for the wear.

I need to get out of here. I got to go. Go. Run.

"Murray! My brothers thought they saw you out there. Did you lose the exact address? If you did, anybody on the block would know which house ours is. You could have knocked on anybody's door."

Louise is at my side, smelling dizzyingly of garlic and spices and meat juices, and then, on her neck: lavender. She laughs as if I said something funny. She straightens my tie. I follow her up the stairs like a lost boy.

She leads me inside to the dining room table, where her father is seated at the head, a man in a neat gray suit with a matching hand-kerchief pressed at his chest. He has the same large head as his sons, a lion's head, with swirls of steel-gray hair. Not a big guy, shorter than his wife and daughter, but I can see where Louise gets her smile. He is smiling at me, sizing me up, lingering on the shoes. Deliberately, he nods, and that gives me enough courage to sit down in the place designated for me next to Louise. The tablecloth is lace, the curtains lace, the fork and knife heavy and silver.

"I need to make introductions," Louise begins. "That's Gino and Vinnie, my younger twin brothers." She sits down into a plastic-covered, red velvet-cushioned seat at her father's right hand, next to me.

"We got it, Louise." Gino grins from across the table, elbowing his brother. "Murray, Jew from the Bronx."

"Is 'Murray' short for Morris or Maurice?" adds Vinnie.

"Is Vinnie short for stupid?" asks Louise.

Gino snorts, and then Vinnie giggles. They jab one another in response. They are twenty-five or so with starched white shirts and collars run wide open to bruiser necks and wafts of cologne.

Their father shoots them a warning look. "Grace first," he says.

"Now that a representative from the chosen people is here," says Gino, who between the two brothers seems to lead the conversation.

"Grace," orders their father.

I bow my head. In grade school, I learned the Lord's Prayer in English and in Latin and can recite it on command. I let my own father's voice bounce around in my head: "Don't be a *luftmensch*, a dreamer. Be a *yiddisher kup*, a smart boy. Speak your lines. They're only lines."

Her father offers grace in a rumbling baritone. At the other side of the table, her mother glares at me and sniffs the air with that nose of hers.

I don't speak.

"Amen," shout her brothers. Her father finishes with a *"Buon appetito,"* and adds, "Good meal, Murray."

Louise nudges me. "So glad you came." Her smell, her perfume, her lavender, is confused with fresh bread, tomatoes, garlic, roasting meat. I haven't eaten a full meal in at least two days.

I shift in my seat. Her father follows my moves with his heavily hooded eyes.

"Everything looks delicious." I bite my lip to keep my stomach from grumbling.

Her brothers snatch up the bread, breaking off the ends with a crack of crust, making a show of it for their father, who winks at them, and then scowls when they don't stop tearing at the bread, breaking it apart between them, spilling seeds everywhere.

"Pass the bread." says Louise. "Now."

Gino or Vinnie hands the loaf over to their mother. I rub my palms down my pants legs.

"Let's serve the lasagna," says her mother to Louise, who rises and disappears into the kitchen. Her mother offers the bread to her husband, who tears off a piece from the middle, more seeds scattering on the white linen tablecloth. I wish the seeds could grow trees of bread.

Before her father places the bread in his mouth, he says, "*Nessun maggior dolore, che ricordarsi del tempo felice, nella miseria.*"

The smell of warm bread rests across the table. I have a strange urge to rip off a chunk and stuff it into my pockets for safekeeping. I keep my hands on my lap.

"Tell Murray what that means," calls out Louise from kitchen.

"How the hell do we know?" asks Gino.

"We don't speak Italian," adds Vinnie.

"They barely speak English," says Louise.

"'There is no greater sorrow than to be mindful of the happy time in misery,'" says her father quietly. "Are you going to serve the lasagna or let the rest of us starve, my daughter?"

"*Libeh iz vi puter, s'iz gut mit brot,*" I find myself mumbling, startling the table, heads turning to me, and I am forced to translate: "Love is sweet, but it's better to have bread with it."

"So, you seek bread over love?" asks her father.

Not that I've had any bread yet, so I shrug.

"Don't worry about my father," says Gino. "He thinks he's descended from Dante."

Louise returns and sees me without bread, gives her brothers the evil eye. I'm not sure they'd call it the evil eye, but I know it when I see it. I carefully tear off a piece the size of my palm, feel the weight of it in my hand and raise it to my lips, savor the smell. I chew slowly so no one will see my hunger.

Louise serves her father a generous corner of the lasagna, layers of noodles, ground meat, cheese, and tomato, and then serves the rest of us.

"*A tavola non si invecchia.* At the table you never become old. Especially with friends and family." He contemplates his plate until Louise shakes a little extra grated cheese across his lasagna. He raises his leonine head at her and says, "Enough. *Grazie.*"

"*Az der mogen iz laidik iz der moi'ech oich laidik.* When the stomach is empty, so is the brain," I murmur to the table's surprise. To my own even.

Her father lowers his forkful of lasagna. "*Mangiare per vivere e non vivere per mangiare.*" He translates succinctly: "Eat to live and live to eat."

"A duel," says Gino.

Her father takes a bite of the lasagna and pronounces it good. Everyone else then raises their forks.

I rack my brain. I am running out of Yiddish sayings that could be repeated in polite company. And the noodles and cheese and meat and sauce, which arrive in beautiful layers on my plate courtesy of Louise, fill my stupid head.

"I'm betting on the old man," says Gino.

"I'll double that bet," says his brother.

Her father pats the corners of his mouth with the linen napkin. *"E quindi uscimmo a riveder le stelle."*

"'And then we came forth, to see again the stars,'" says Louise, grinning. Her mother shoots her a watery evil eye.

"Let's end this on the *Divine Comedy. Manga.* Eat," says her father, returning to his lasagna.

Before I eat, I observe how they cut into the noodles, a slice off the end as if it's sweet, not savory, a careful bend to the fork to keep the noodles on, the sauce suspended on the utensil. Do they know that traditional Jews do not mix meat and dairy? But I am not traditional, far from it.

Her mother points her knife at me. "We also have a nice roast beef. You can eat that, right?"

"I eat everything."

"I see that," she says, indicating my lasagna.

"Louise, can you bring in the roast?" asks her mother.

Louise jumps up and disappears back into the kitchen, returning after a few moments of silence at the table with a sizzling piece of meat wrapped in string and oozing juices.

Her mother waves a carving knife, as if she has been waiting for her chance at the meat all afternoon. "Gentle with that roast, Louise."

Before letting the knife touch the meat, her mother sharpens its blade on a whetstone with a swish and a thwack, striking the knife against the stone, one side and then the other with hypnotic purpose and intent. "Giuseppe!" she finally says. She thrusts the knife in front of her husband, indicating that he should carve. He waves her off.

"Mama always carves," whispers Louise into my ear.

In her mother's hands, the roast is sliced paper-thin, pink in the middle, perfection in meat. She could have fed ten families with that one roast.

"More lasagna?" Louise asks me.

"In Korea, I ate *kimchi*. That's spicy cabbage," I say to Louise as she serves me more. "They ferment it in the ground."

"We don't eat foreign food here." Louise's mother seals her lips in distaste.

"I don't know why we even bothered with Korea. I would have dropped the bomb on them too," says Gino.

"Can we not talk about bombs or missiles, Ma?"

"My daughter doesn't talk about her work," said her mother, aiming her knife at Louise's direction and mine.

"She's in the Army," explains Gino. "She didn't tell you? It's only an office job. She don't get a gun."

"I'm a clerk-typist. At the Brooklyn Navy Yard. I also translate. Italian. German. Some Spanish."

"I'm impressed," I say, thinking, *I can't eat anymore. I should get up and leave.*

"I'm glad somebody is," she says, squeezing my hand under the table.

"Everything she types is classified" says Gino.

"She don't tell us nothing," adds Vinnie.

"Those are the rules, and there are some rules that need to be followed," says Louise.

"Rules are for fools," says Gino.

Vinnie munches on a chunk of lasagna; the sauce drizzles down his chin as he laughs at his brother's wit.

His mother stops carving and glares at her sons. Vinnie raises his heavy cloth napkin from his lap slowly and theatrically, and scrubs at his chin. She serves her husband the roast first, making a show of being particular with what slice to put on his plate.

"We're both engaged," says Gino to me. His mother piles a generous helping of the roast to his plate.

"They've been engaged for the past four years, Murray," says Louise.

"Our girls, they're sisters. They want to wait until they're twenty." Gino wrestles his knife and fork into the meat on his plate.

"Yeah, like that's some magical age to get married, right, Louise?" asks Vinnie.

"What do you do, Murray?" asks Louise's mother.

"How do you like your meat?" asks Louise of me.

On my plate, I want to answer.

"How about rare?" she asks, and I nod.

"I asked him what does he do? Does he answer me?"

I drive a taxicab when I need money, a sub, fill-in, in the middle of the night for a guy my father knows. Mainly I play basketball, or if it it's raining, I walk over to the public library and read and read and read, the newspapers, or history books. So I say to Louise's mother, "I'm studying to be a teacher. At NYU. On the GI Bill."

"See? A teacher, Ma."

"Teachers don't make much money," her mother says, her fork and knife poised over her own piece of well-done roast beef. "What kind of work is your father in?"

"Chickens."

Her brothers snicker.

"He owns a farm," I explain. "A chicken farm in New Jersey."

"A farm?" The nose rises in the air and the back straightens. "And you live in the Bronx?"

"Across from Crotona Park. My father's cousin owns the building. He's moved up to Westchester. But I still live there."

"The one thing you can say about the Jews," says her mother, pointing her knife at her sons.

"Please don't say it," says Louise.

"They invest their money well," her mother continues. "Not in the horses. Not in the numbers. Not like some people I know."

"Ma," says Louise.

Her father pats his lips with the linen napkin.

"At least he lives in his family's building," says her mother.

"Ma!"

"Family," replies her mother.

"Our sister is moving to Greenwich Village. Did she tell you?" Gino elbows Vinnie. "Our sister is going to Hell," adds Gino. "Right, Ma? Straight to Hell."

"Enough," says Louise's father.

The bread is passed again from one brother to another, and torn again, and passed and torn again.

"Bread?" Louise says to me. She yanks what is left of the loaf away from Gino, offering it to me. I take it.

"What did I do?" Gino swipes the scattering of tomato sauce on his plate with his chunk of Italian bread. He shoves the heel into his mouth.

I chew and study the thin cracks in the wall over the brothers' heads, the filaments of time. Think of the word "filaments."

Louise is watching me. Her mother has me in her sights too. "A farm?"

"Murray?" said Louise. "Maybe you'd like some more lasagna? Is the roast beef okay?"

I take another bite, thinking I could eat the whole roast. "Yes, thank you."

"Airport is out this way," Gino says, tearing at his meat. "Idlewild. I work there. Airline mechanic for Pan Am. Vinnie does the same thing, for Eastern. That's the future." He says this to his father as much as to me and shoves more meat into his mouth.

His father shrugs. "The future?"

"Moving fast, Papa. Airplanes. Jets. Rockets."

"*Vino,*" says the father. "Wine. That is the future and the past. Why didn't anyone bring the wine to the table? Is this what this family has come to?"

"I'll get it," says Louise, glaring at her brothers.

After the wine appears, glistening in a cut-glass carafe, Louise pours her father a glass, then travels around the table and pours everyone a full glass, except her mother, who waves her hand in front of her glass and says, "Just a drop."

"*Salut,*" says her father, raising his glass.

"*Salut,*" repeat the sons and hurry the wine to their lips.

"*Salut,*" whispers Louise next to me, touching her lips to the glass.

The wine glints in the cut crystal. I haven't even had time to swallow and raise mine. I go for the wine.

"Wait!" says her father, addressing me. "What's your word?"

"'My word'?"

"You raise your glass, what do the Jews say?"

This deep-red wine smells full of body and earth; it is as thick or thicker than blood.

"*L'Chayim.*" I hold my wineglass with both hands. And I add, "to life."

"*L'Chayim,*" he repeats. His wife glares at him. "To a *long*, prosperous and fruitful life," he says. He finishes off the wine and pours another glass.

After the dinner and more wine and desserts, including a sweet cream in a delicate shell. "A cannoli," Louise says, before she picks up the shell with her fingers and licks the cream with the tip of her tongue. I imitate her, clumsily breaking apart the crust, misting sugar on my fingers and shirt and pants.

"This was all, all…" I must search for the word. "Delicious. Thank you."

Her mother accepts this compliment with another sniff.

"We loved having you," says Louise.

"I have class in the morning," I lie. "At NYU." I push my chair back from the dining room table.

Her father raises his wineglass to me.

Her brothers nod. "We got to go too. Our girls are waiting, and we don't like to keep them waiting too long," says Gino.

They kiss their mother on the cheek, and then their father. I don't know when I kissed my father last; it must be at least twenty years ago.

"I'll walk with you to the bus." Louise leans toward me. "I want to kiss that sugar off your lips."

I swipe the napkin across my lips, all the time Louise watching me, and her mother watching her. I say my goodbyes to her father and mother and brothers, and at least her father offers his hand. Her mother waves me off.

Louise informs her parents to "Leave the dishes. I'll do them when I come back," and guides me out the door with me before her mother can say no.

On her front stoop, the late afternoon light lies against the cemetery, and the graveyard's towering trees and mausoleums and tombstones glisten in the late afternoon sun. They are lucky, these dead, to have this place.

Louise bounds down the stairs.

"Let's go," she says, crossing the street without looking, climbing over the low wall into the cemetery. "It's a shortcut to the express bus," she explains when I hesitate.

We pass the headstones of angels praying or pleading, their faces upturned; we pass crypts where entire families look like they're buried, and graves, too many to count, birthdates and death dates blurred on the stone. On some, only one name is etched and the space left blank for another, usually the wife.

Some girls will keep talking at you no matter what, but not Louise. She lets the quiet be quiet.

We find ourselves on a hill with as perfect a view of the Manhattan skyline as exists in the world. We are the only ones standing. This is the most isolated corner of New York City I have ever been to in my life.

"Doesn't this feel close to Heaven?" she asks and opens her arms wide like she will take in the whole cemetery, the fields, the sky. She spins and strokes the face of one of the angels.

"I have to get back to the Bronx."

"Don't you believe in Heaven?"

"Jews don't talk about Heaven."

"Why not?"

"Just doesn't come up."

Louise considers this point. "What do you believe will happen?"

She strides over to where the graves end, to a low rock wall, something handmade, the rocks uneven, something old, probably dating back to the Revolutionary War when this part of Queens was farmland. If she tumbles over the wall, she will hit a main cemetery road, a dirt road, and then into a row of wood houses clutching the side of the hill, and a factory or an auto shop at the very bottom, and the creek, black with oil, and the surging East River beyond that. I believe all that could happen, if she goes over the wall.

Across the East River, the sun sets behind the spire of the Chrysler Building. We are the only ones here, talking and breathing.

"Luck," I say, causing her to turn back to me. "Randomness. I believe some of us live and some of us don't, and we don't know why." The scent of the river and the auto shops and expressway roils the spring air, oil and gas and burning plastic and metals and waste. Two hawks circle.

"I think I believe."

"You think?"

"Until proven otherwise."

I'm not sure if she is being straight with me or not. Her face is raised to the setting sun. She is resting against a family tomb with its angel high above her head. Behind her, the tomb is above ground; an inch or two of Italian marble is set along the flat top. It's as if the family knew that you'd need a place to sit if you found yourself at the edge of Queens.

"Come here," she says.

"We should get going, if we don't want to be here after the sun sets."

"The sun isn't setting so soon," she says.

The light lazes across the tombstones, against the family vaults, against their inscriptions, caskets, bones. I look down and find a smooth, perfectly round stone. Jews mark visits to cemeteries with stones placed on headstones—not that I'm visiting anyone here in this Roman Catholic cemetery.

I twirl the round, cool stone across my fingers and sit down on the slab next to her. She rubs the side of my face with her knuckles. I grow cold inside, the kind of cold I can't easily shake.

Her knuckles drag down my face to my shoulder and arm. "Hello? Murray?"

"Maybe this should be goodbye.? Maybe I should get going."

"Murray."

Her eyes don't leave mine.

"I should get going. You can't get from Maspeth to the Bronx, not easily."

"I know," she says. It breaks through again—her smile, a big, glorious smile.

"Louise, I think we should say we had a nice time—dancing—and I appreciate the dinner. You're a nice girl."

"I'm moving to the Village, Murray. Greenwich Village with my girlfriend Marlene. At the end of the month. My parents aren't stopping me. Nice Italian girls get married and have children. Nice Italian girls go to confession every week. Nice Italian girls don't bring home a Jew from the Bronx. So why did I?"

Over our heads, the hawks swoop. I feel like we are the only people alive in New York City, but this can't be. There are millions in the city doing what they do: driving cabs, walking a beat, playing ball, feeding the kids, getting ready for work on Monday, living lives that I'm looking through the window at—yet Louise and I have found ourselves alone.

Her wide brown eyes take in the hawks and the sky. They fly off like they're dancing on the winds. And I cover her mouth with my own and kiss her now. I taste the sweet cannoli cream.

After a moment, I pull away. "I think you're a nice Italian girl."

"Nice? My parents want me to be nice. My brothers. My office." Louise strokes the sides of my face. "I hear that song playing in my head."

"What song?"

She starts to sing the song the band was playing right before the police raid, "Save The Last Dance for Me." She is badly off-key. I can't help it, I laugh.

"What the hell," she says and reaches for my waist.

My hand cups her hand.

"Hello, Murray? Another kiss?" she says. "Or I'll start singing again."

I press her body to mine and find her mouth with my own. I think I am made for a girl like this—tall and solid and laughing and tasting like sweet cream. She kicks her shoes off and strokes her legs up and down my own. She laughs at nothing and makes me laugh at nothing, and everything.

She slips her glasses into her handbag. I rub the stone with my thumb for luck.

My lips travel over the length of her and into the folds of her pink shirt. She opens the buttons.

She kisses each side of my face. "I love these dimples. They break apart the seriousness of you." She knows joy. "I was hoping for a kiss, Murray, but I'm okay with more."

"Are you sure?" Sweat breaks out cold along my back.

"No one ever comes into the cemetery at this time of day."

"I should go."

"Lie on the grass with me." She doesn't wait. She stretches down to the green at the edge of the cemetery. She rolls down her nylons to her toes and flicks off the stockings too. Her legs are bare.

I remove my only suit jacket and drop it next to her pocketbook. She eases onto my jacket, and I am soon next to her, and she is running her hands over my shoulders, up my neck, into my hair. I want to apologize for not getting a haircut.

She whispers, "Save the last dance for me." I draw her to me. She is tall and strong, but I am taller and stronger. I hold her tight, and she holds me tighter. And sometimes the kiss is all of itself; no words are needed. I find hips, warm and wide, and she finds my chest inside my shirt and rubs hard like I have good luck to spare. She peels off the pink blouse. Unpins her hair. I rip off my tie. I have a US Army-issued condom from Korea in my wallet and use it, letting my stone rest next to us for a moment and then returning it to my hand, hoping she doesn't see this transaction.

Exposed to the vast, dusky sky, to the furious heat of her hands over my shoulders, we find ourselves on the grass, my flush face against the crook of her arm, and I duck for cover in her breasts.

She smiles at the sky and says, "Hello, Murray," when I enter her, forgetting where I am for a moment, feeling only her arms and legs wrap around me, and me aching for her touch. I dig my palms into the dirt to steady us. Straight ahead, the hawks swoop back and circle.

Afterward, we walk along the edge of the cemetery hill. She takes my hand and discovers my stone, and we walk the stone in both of our hands. The sunset etches Manhattan in embers, smothering into smoke and haze, into dusk, into city night.

"You're going to need to get this suit cleaned." She kisses me again on my cheek and ear.

"You do this with other guys?"

"Like I said, you're the first one... I ever invited to dinner."

"The first?" I tease.

"Should I ask you about your first time? Or should you just shut up and kiss me again?"

She doesn't wait; she kisses me.

•

That week, I get a haircut. I scrub the apartment with bleach. I return all the books to the public library. I use my GI benefits to sign up for summer classes at NYU, determined to finish my degree.

On Sunday morning, my parents make the long trek back into the Bronx. They drive up in their white delivery truck and carry down into my basement apartment shopping bags of food: roasted chicken, boiled potatoes and carrots, and *hamentashen* with raspberry and apricot and poppy seed, the latter of which wedges in between my teeth and gives me the ever-slight euphoria of its original plant. My mother presses my suit and asks no questions. My father argues with me to return with them to the chicken farm. I want to tell them about Louise; however, I've already decided never to see Louise again. My father places twenty dollars under the stone he finds on my dresser. After my parents leave, I put the stone and the money in my pocket. I go shoot hoops in the park until I can't see the net in the dark, until my heart stops with each thud of the ball, until I can taste the sweat in the back of my throat like tears.

Leaving Maspeth

My mother circles me. "I never wanted to leave. I was born in a speck of a village outside Palermo, and I would have stayed there forever if your father hadn't played cards with my papa and won."

At the kitchen table, my father lifts his shoulders from his newspapers, the whole upper half of his body, as if an emotion that wasn't quite happy or sad had been plucked out of him, so classically Italian I have to rush over and hug him. He has a broad face and a sweep of thick gray hair and shares a smile when I come to him. He's dressed on this Saturday morning like he's expecting company, but that's how he always dresses: a pressed white handkerchief in his shirt pocket, a white shirt with extra starch, licorice suckers in his pocket to soothe his throat.

He whispers to me, "And I will never regret it because I have you."

"It's no good for you to leave," my mother continues, ignoring us. "I'm telling you, Louise, you're not going anywhere."

"I have it all set with Marlene."

She stares at me, and I stare right back. "I don't like this," she says. "Do you hear me, Joe? I don't like this."

"I hear you, Carolina. Everyone hears you." He turns the page of his *Daily Racing Form*.

"How do you know this girl? Tell me again."

"Ma."

"She's not from the neighborhood."

"No."

"Where's she from?"

"The painting class."

"She thinks she's an artist too?"

"She's a secretary, an executive assistant," I say, wishing I knew more about Marlene, who I met when I took my one and only painting class in the Village. But I'm not going to admit this to my mother.

"Does she type a hundred words a minute like you?"

"I don't know, Ma."

"Does she work for the United States Army like you?"

"No."

"So, you don't know her family."

"Does it matter? I'm not moving in with her family."

"Now maybe you can tell your mother this. Will you see him again?"

"Who?"

"Who else? The man in the moon? That Jew from the Bronx. He shows up and eats my roast, my lasagna, two servings of each, and you don't hear from him again, or have you?"

I haven't heard from Murray since Sunday dinner three weeks ago. It doesn't matter. I am moving out.

"He's too good for you? Is that what he thinks? You are my daughter, and you are too good for him! Never. Not my daughter. Not to a Jew from the Bronx. You don't worry. Your father and I have been talking."

"We have?" says my father. "What have we been saying?"

"Ma!"

"Tell me this, where is he from?"

"The Bronx, you just said it."

"He's from somewhere," says my mother. "Or his family was from somewhere. Nobody just shows up in the Bronx. A man like that has history on his back."

She spits, warding off evil, men, the dust in the air, cursing it all, the devil too. And I have to smile, I just have to, and she doesn't like that either. She releases a string of curses in Italian so ferocious, so Sicilian, it makes me laugh. She screams at me, at the ceiling, at the air closing in around the three of us.

"What's all this?" asks my father. "What are you saying? You know what you're saying? You're going to bring down the house on us all."

"Your daughter is leaving, and I've got to tell her something."

"You can put all the curses you want on my head, I'm going. It's time," I tell her.

My mother pinches my arm to make sure I am paying attention. "I put the curse on him, not you. Don't answer if he calls you. You can do better. Or you'll come home to us and that will be that. We'll call the cousins in. We'll get you married to a nice Italian boy, won't we, Joe?"

"I should go find my deck of cards," says her father, only half joking.

My mother presses a pan of her lasagna on me. She might not want me to go but she isn't going to let me go hungry. She makes me promise that I'll be home for Sunday dinner next week. She'll excuse me for tomorrow. My brothers' fiancées are coming anyway.

She plants her watery eyes on me, another curse swelling in the bloodshot irises. "Go! Go without my blessings. Without them, you hear me? And make sure you bring back my lasagna pan clean."

I leave. I take the late-morning express bus into Manhattan. I dress in my matching new spring coat and pillbox hat and patent leather pocketbook. I tease my hair into a flip. I am leaving Maspeth in style with my pan of lasagna. My father accompanies me to the bus stop, carrying my bags. My mother had brushed his fedora, and he wears it cocked over one eye. He'll go to the track later, bet on the horses, win hopefully but lose most likely, yet now he is reaching up to kiss my forehead, his eyes full of tears, as if I am taking a long journey and not a short trip across the bridge and downtown to Greenwich Village.

•

Marlene's apartment is above Bruno's Spaghetti Shop on Bleecker. Steam pumps from the shop, and it's like clouds are being made for this street only. A flock of chatty pigeons whirls over the hiss and heat. A lineup of beat-up metal garbage cans festers along the sidewalk. Her apartment is on the top floor, the third floor, a walk-up. I make two trips with my suitcases and shopping bags. All the while, the pigeons peck at me like they own the place.

At the door, Marlene kisses me, both cheeks, lightly, like she is all of a sudden French. She leads me through a front room, with each wall painted a different color— yellow, sea green, black and tomato red—and a lush, creamy, sleek burnt-orange couch. Leaning against the walls, opposite the couch, are unframed paintings four or five feet tall—splashes of color and not much else. The ceiling is painted sky blue. I almost expect to see frescos. I remember: my mother's house is white, inside and out, and it's like I never knew it until now.

"You like the art?" asks Marlene, wrapping her arms around my waist. "Abstract. I bought it in Washington Square. There was this art fair all along the streets. That's what I love about the Village. You go out for a newspaper and there's art. I *hondled* the guy down to get two for the price of one." She swings around me.

On the windowsill, more pigeons cluck and patter. "Nesting." Marlene's eyelids are rimmed with black eyeliner, Elizabeth Taylor's Cleopatra eyes. The rest of her face is bare. She wears a bright green and white kimono-style bathrobe and her breasts bounce when she walks. Outside the kitchen window, laundry lines crisscross the alley. A half-dozen or so white shirts flap in the breeze. More pigeons perch between the clean shirts. She doesn't offer to take my coat or hat.

"So, you're here." Marlene eases against the window ledge in the living room, lighting a cigarette, swirling her smoke, abstractly as the paintings. "I need first and last months' rent right away. And I want us to have a party immediately."

"A party?" I never had a party that didn't include my brothers, their fiancées, my aunts and uncles and cousins and their kids and in-laws and people you weren't sure how they were related.

"We'll invite some people I know, only the cool, hip and very single ones. I know some musicians and a few people in the neighborhood. We'll just spin some records, get some jugs of wine, and, to paraphrase Ginsberg, we will jump off the roof to solitude! Waving! Carrying flowers! Down to the river! Into the street!"

Pigeons flutter and squawk toward the sun. The windows are bare, curtain-less. A breeze steals in. The streaking sunlight flashes off the walls. I don't know the poet or the poem.

"Why don't you take your coat and hat off and stay a while? You know, I met a guy that night too," Marlene says. "He walked me all the way home from Howard Johnson's after the Palladium was raided, and I think he expected—well, I know what he expected, but I was ruined by then. I didn't need him to bury me. You never heard from your guy that night, did you? What's his name again?"

I could be coy, say, "What guy?" But I don't feel young enough to be coy. I don't take my coat or hat off. Maybe I'm not going to stay.

Marlene says his name. "Murray Blech, right?"

"He came for Sunday dinner."

"He did? Tell."

I will not confess to Marlene.

"There's nothing more to tell, is there?" she asks. She studies me. "Sex? Did you have sex? You can see I like saying that word. S-e-x. And I can see you're blushing, or what is that contortion, a new dance? Nothing happened, did it? Did you ever hear from him again?"

"Give me a cigarette. Please, Marlene."

"Don't feel like you have to entertain me or answer to me at all. That's the fun of living with me."

I take a few hurried puffs, and I don't like the taste. I jam it out in a glass ashtray with the Palladium Ballroom inscribed on it.

"You have beautiful brown eyes." Marlene sighs so close to me I can taste her cigarette. "We'll share the bedroom unless one of us has a reason not to share, and then that one could sleep on the couch for a night or two. Lumpy. Uncomfortable. But it will do you, angel." She blows a long stream of smoke toward the window. The pigeons don't seem to mind.

"You know, Louise, I like city birds." Marlene yawns, tipping her neck, running her hand down the length of her throat and back up into the velvety hair. "What else?" she asks. "What do you like?" Her kimono splays open. Her legs are creamy and flawless.

I spin around. Where am I going to put all my things, the lasagna my mother packed for me? In the kitchen, a dwarf refrigerator and a stove with two gas burners and an oven are jammed together alongside a table with two mismatching chairs. "I like late nights over early mornings," I say, unbuttoning my coat, suddenly warm, and placing it over the back of the chair.

"Really?" Marlene laughs, with a bite of sarcasm. I plan on practicing that laugh.

"Sometimes." I plan on staying up all night, something I've never done. I try again. "I like tall men."

"What else? And that one from the Palladium." She whistles like a man. "He looked underfed, lean, if I'm being polite, and those hands—big hands."

I can't help it; I blush. "A decent dancer."

"Is that all?" Marlene flicks her ash out the window. "So tell me, angel, what else do you like? I need to know. And I get the bathroom first. It's just a tub. No shower, I hope that's okay? At least it's not in the kitchen." Pigeons screech and flutter across the alley. Marlene skims her tongue over her small white teeth. "I feed them bread crumbs so they'll come by every morning. What else? What else do you like?"

"Sinatra vs. Elvis." I run my hands over the walls and marvel at my palms when the colors don't streak off. I have this strange desire to lick the walls to see if the yellow tastes like lemon. "It's a big thing in Maspeth, who you like more."

"I'm sure it is," says Marlene, rising from the windowsill and crossing the short distance from the living room to the kitchen. "I need more coffee. You?" There are only dregs left in the pot, so I decline. She digs a cup out of the dirty dishes in the sink and gives it a quick rinse. My mother would be shocked by the—how many? three spoons of sugar Marlene adds to her black coffee. She eases into one of the kitchen chairs.

"Folk music, that's what's in now," says Marlene. "Gerde's Folk City is right down the block."

"Oh. Or, cool. It's *cool*, right?" I feel like I am practicing another language.

"If you want. Cool or groovy."

"Groovy? *Groovy*. I want to say 'gravy' for some reason."

Marlene laughs so hard she must hold her kimono closed. "What else, Louise?"

"I like JFK."

This point causes Marlene to pluck my pillbox hat off my head. She places it on the edge of her head, but it doesn't stay, sliding down the side of her angular face. "You know nobody wears hats like this down here except the tourists or Jackie Kennedy when she comes to visit. We should go shopping. Get you a very black beret, and angel, whatever happened to that red dress I let you borrow? You should wear that every day. Anything but pillboxes and polka dots, which make you look old, and I'm saying this because we are going to living together, angel. You don't want to look old around here."

I accept my hat back and stick it behind me on the countertop. I want a silk kimono. I want everything that Marlene seems to have so easily.

"Don't get me wrong, honey. I voted for JFK too. I couldn't vote for that sweaty Richard Nixon." Marlene shudders playfully.

"I'm old. Thirty-two," I say and stop. We had been talking about Nixon, hadn't we?

"That's old? How old do you think I am?"

I always assumed that she is younger than me. Everyone is younger than me.

"I'm thirty-six in May," says Marlene. "But I'll deny that in public. Whose business is it? If anyone asks, I'm twenty-six, and you should be too. How about more coffee?"

Marlene scoops up coffee grounds, stretches out of the window, and scatters them into a row of seedlings, which are lined up on the fire escape. "Better still, how about a glass of wine?"

"Too early."

"It's after noon, isn't it?" From out of the dwarf refrigerator, a bottle of Chianti—from atop the refrigerator, two jelly glasses. She reaches into one of my shopping bags and places my mother's lasagna between us. She peels it open, like skin, eating only the cheese first, then the pasta strips, the bits of burnt garlic.

"I have to unpack." I am precise about my things. For everything there is a place, but I don't say this to Marlene.

Marlene fills the jelly glasses to the brim with the Chianti. A few drops splash me, and she picks up my hand and with a wicked sweep of her tongue licks off the wine. "Drink," she says.

I stare at my hand. She finishes off her wine like a good girl downing her morning milk. I drink too. Sounds of the street pulse into the apartment: a screeching far-off bus, a plucking guitar, the clank of garbage cans opened and closed, shouts from the neighbors—mumbled Italian—a bit of wind and the stirring of pigeons —all at once they rustle into flight. The sun dapples the colored walls, blending by a trick of the eye into other colors, and Marlene stands up suddenly, catching me around the shoulders, twirling into my lap with bony hips, ordering me to drink wine, and I do. The colors in the room blur together like a finger painting. We are all light.

Marlene rests her head on my shoulders. For a second, I imagine that she is going to kiss me full on. Instead, she flings her head back, hums a few bars of nothing I recognize, and I hold her steady.

"I have to unpack, to undress, or change," I say even though what I really want is to be kissed. I had wanted to be kissed back at the cemetery, and I was. I wanted the sky over me. I wanted the opposite of death, and somehow Murray knew that. I stand up.

"I started clearing out two dresser drawers and half the closet for you," says Marlene, swirling away. "It's a mess but no one will see it but us."

I hurry toward the bedroom.

"Come back soon," calls Marlene. "I miss you already."

•

When I return, a half hour or so later, Marlene is smoking a cigarette down to its very end. The last of the smoke drifts from her nose and lips. "So, when should we have our first party, Louise?"

"As soon as possible."

The party is the following Saturday night and, according to Marlene, "Everyone is here."

I don't know anyone.

I'm in new black capri pants and flats, which are almost too small, and I feel bloated and swollen with cheap wine. After an hour crammed into the apartment, I escape to the roof.

Glass crushes under my steps. An abandoned pigeon coop, blanched wood and rusted wires scraped against the black roof tar, is positioned in one corner. The party beats out the windows one floor below: a girl singer's stringy voice, a guitar, and bongos. A crowd gathers on Marlene's fire escape—arms and legs dangle over the street. Someone recites poetry. Nobody listens. The party caves into the hall; it is midnight, and all the boys and girls, Marlene's friends, are murmuring and clucking and bumping into one another, the quietest noisy party I have ever been to in my life.

On the roof, I lean into what breeze I can find. Everything about me feels insubstantial, out of body.

I drop my wineglass, and it soars off the roof into the utter darkness. After a second—*crash*. Flapping wings zigzag over the roof.

"Whoa," he says, coming up behind me. "Like a bomb. Bam. And then nothing."

The bongos bounce to the roof. Someone sings out louder than before, screeching high notes. Everyone is younger than me at the party. Marlene had ironed my hair flat down to my shoulders and cut bangs across my forehead. She insisted on lending me a sleeveless turtleneck, black and skintight, and said that pants looked on me exactly how they should look. I had to pry my glasses from her; she said they ruined my look.

"Did you notice? Nobody noticed," he says. "Just you and me."

He rests against the roof's edge as if older, his spidery legs stretched in front of him, his back to the moon, a full moon. He has a guitar with him and slants it to his side. He is sipping a beer, straight from the bottle. His jeans are old, or at least torn at the knees, his shirt too wide for his shoulders and of a color I had never seen on a man—orange-red like a hot day's sunset. He has too much hair, tufts, wooly, all over his head, and he's comfortable with it, like he wants it to look this way, or doesn't care.

His shoes—because I always notice a man's shoes—are scuffed-up brown leather boots. I've never known a man who wore such boots, cowboy boots. I've never liked Westerns, never had John Wayne or Lone Ranger fantasies of being roped or steered. Never traveled farther west than New Jersey, and I'm not sure it is considered west of anything but Manhattan.

I don't bother with a smile.

"Jonathan," he says. He judges where to place the beer bottle on the ledge, picking up the guitar with a stroke down its neck, then a fast riff, then slow, bluesy and aching, and then nothing, air, as if his hands are thinking. His fingers pluck a few strings: slow, fast, and searching. He ruffles back his hair when he doesn't find what he wanted.

"Louise. Louise Garofalo."

He strums again as if he'd forgotten me.

I pace toward the dented metal door. I'm going down to find more wine and someone my age to talk with tonight.

He makes my name a song. "Lo-o-o-o-Louise." He strums. "I play at clubs, Louise, but mostly make my money in Washington Square Park on Saturdays and Sundays. I was once a miner, and my parents are dead, and one of my uncles plays harmonica and another was the best pickpocket in Chicago. I joined the carnival at seventeen or so and traveled with it through the Midwest. One day I hitchhiked east to visit another uncle, the musical one, amazing. He can mimic any tune he hears on his harmonica. He's in an insane asylum in Jersey. A friend from the club told me about the party."

"How old are you?"

"Twenty or so."

His fingers work through the music, finding a piece and pulling ahead, then back. His hair falls into his eyes. He lights a cigarette. After a few minutes, the tobacco burns down to his lips. He flicks the butt off the roof.

I pull my glasses off so all the city spins into a blur of light and stars and a moon pinned behind his head. I squint at him and decide I need my glasses back on.

He glances over and says, "Please keep them off."

He is such a baby. He's ten—no, what did he say? Twelve years younger.

"I'm going back down to the party," I say, firmly replacing my cat's-eye glasses.

He leaps in front of me and bows as if the cowboy had become a knight, as if anyone could change that easily. "Great eyes," he says, and his fingers, extra-long, delicate, slip my glasses off and tuck them away in his orange-red shirt pocket. "Flecks of gold and green in them. Please look at me. I followed you up here. This isn't an accident."

Callused thumbs smear my red lipstick across my face. I touch the puffs of his hair, waving thick over his frayed collar. I swallow hard. Men don't wear their hair like this in Maspeth, Queens.

He hums scales, on key. "I suppose you want me to stop?" he asks after a set.

Anybody could come up, but nobody has so far. "I hope I live to see a man on the moon," he says.

The moon or New Jersey seems closer than before. "I won't live that long."

"Why not?" He traces his hand over my turtleneck, over my nipples, and back up and over again.

He stretches out on the roof tar. "Join me on this beach?" He slips out of his shirt without unbuttoning it. His chest and shoulders are hairless and so like a boy, so unlike Murray's. He is still talking about the moon as he lays his shirt out for me. "Before we put a man on the moon, we should understand other things first, like perfect pitch."

The moon is so close. I should sit.

"God is like perfect pitch. Did you ever think of that?"

"No."

He strums, his chest rising.

I don't want to admit that I am pretty sure I'm tone deaf.

"I'm saying there are theories about perfect pitch," he says. "Now can you please take off that shirt before your breasts make me go as crazy as my uncle?"

I pull off Marlene's turtleneck. His mouth finds the valley between my breasts and buzz what I assume is a perfect note, though I am distracted by his lips.

He doesn't have to talk, just kiss.

He clips off my bra.

I reassure myself: I want this. He considers my bra: plain, white, with extra support, nothing fancy. It's as if someone else's bra is getting tossed over the roof and into the night, someone else's dark red nipples are bare on the rooftop, someone else's crescent stomach.

"I have a theory about notes too. Chords too," he goes on. "I write music, and then it's like someone else wrote it. But it's that first perfect note that starts everything."

The streetlamps throw light everywhere but on this corner of the roof. "What do you think?"

I kiss him. He has said enough.

"How about this, then?" he says after the kiss that tasted of too many cigarettes and a few beers. "The Bible says that the world was made in six days."

"Enough."

"I say the universe was made after the first perfect note." He pecks at my neck, once, twice, humming, stopping to think another big thought. "Maybe He just opened his mouth, breathed, and thought about the note."

He clears his throat and releases another note. "And that was the end of God."

Pigeons coo in their perches along the ledge.

"Thoughts?" he asks. He's challenging me like a boy would. "About perfect pitch?" He sings a few more notes out loud. I'm sure they are perfect enough.

I don't want to argue about God, or perfect pitch, or even men on the moon with this singing boy. I smother his mouth with mine. He sings to himself or to me, or to the pigeons.

"Can you help me?" he asks, almost in song.

I am grateful for something to do. I'm always better with a task at hand, a project. I slide his jeans off, down to his ankles, and yank the boots off, and his socks stink, so I take them off too. His legs are downy, covered in fine soft hairs. He stretches out like he likes being free of his things. He stares above my head, toward New Jersey, and the white blur of the moon skinning the night sky.

"How about this: that moon is like looking at the face of God. What sounds do you think are on the moon?"

"If I only knew."

"Enough?" he says. His flat midwestern accent comes through with that one word: enough. "Of me or God?" he asks.

His God must be from the Midwest too. "Enough."

"Listen," he says, drawing himself to me, bending me back. "Press your ear against my chest." And I do, and he hums into my ear, a howl, then an echo of a howl. I lie back on his orange-red shirt as he howls over me.

"The moon, baby," he says.

I peer over his shock of hair and see how the moon frames his slight shoulders. I want to get up. I can hear voices, and I am sure they were coming up to the roof. But instead I shudder. He is inside me. I am being made love to on a roof above Bruno's Spaghetti Shop in Greenwich Village, and I can smell flour baking.

His knees are soon black with roof tar. His hand strokes near my mouth. I suck on his knuckles and fingers. He says, "Go easy." That hair of his falls over his face and mine. He skips a note, finds another and holds it in his mouth while he finishes with me, pulling out at the end, hot against my leg. Then he surprises me, starts again slowly, closing his eyes, until the song he'd been creating in the back of his throat settles in his rib cage.

And Jonathan is much less careful the second time. He stretches over me, and I can see the moon straight up and hear him humming to the back of my neck until he rolls over, yanking on his jeans, gathering his guitar and tucking my glasses back on my head. He has a gig in Philadelphia, he is telling me. I only know that "gig" means that he is going. I reach for him, but he is double-checking that he has everything: pants, wallet, the moon at his back. He kisses me quick on the mouth, runs his hand over my lips one more time. This time I open my mouth. Taste the salt in his skin one more time. I have to stand up too. He needs his shirt.

"Imagine if you could stay forever young," he says.

I am naked on the roof, broader and fleshier than he is, taller too. I can't tell him now that I am beyond being forever young.

He looks past me. "Perfect pitch is God, I'm sure of it now. My gift to you." He says he promised these friends of his that he'd meet them at their club, catch the last set. He says I am cool, very cool and beautiful, and I feel neither, but it's nice for him to say it. He departs the roof in a trail of notes.

The party continues all night. I tug on the turtleneck and the capris without my bra or underpants. Dawn arrives over Seventh Avenue and West Fourth in shadows more than light. Blood pounds in my head and chest. A guitar is being strummed from somewhere, and I follow the music, thinking I'll find Jonathan, but he was true to his word.

•

Weeks later, the end of July, a Saturday night, I'm in new clothes: a billowy gold blouse, which rounds my neck and pulls easily off my shoulders; a full black Gypsy skirt with an elastic waist; a dab of Marlene's French perfume. I powder my throat. Sweat beads on my neck. The apartment is stifling, without a breeze or a stir in the three rooms. Even the pigeons are silenced in the heat. I pin my hair up, slash the red lipstick across my lips, the lipstick mine.

No staying in, watching the television tonight. Marlene is visiting her family tonight, a rare visit. I need to get out. I need to search one last time for Jonathan. I have circled through Washington Square Park a dozen times. I have waited under that arch for hours, smoking cigarette after cigarette, following the pings of guitars and the shushes of chess players. I have watched college kids kiss or inhale, or inhale and kiss, and others strum. I have observed how the chess players slide a bishop, jump a knight, inch along a queen, a king; how they slap down stop clocks and reset boards.

Tonight, I will look for Jonathan one more time. I've heard he's gone off to Boston, is on the road, another gig. Or I've also heard he is right here in Manhattan, in midtown or uptown, or maybe in Los Angeles, cutting an album. Did one cut an album or lay down tracks or both? I need someone to translate for me, or, more simply, I need to find him.

In Marlene's mirror, I feel bound and loose at the same time. I turn—the hips are a little wider, and the breasts, rounder. In this outfit, however, I don't look pregnant at all.

Marlene had given me the name of a nurse who performed abortions in her West Village apartment once a month. It had to be on a Sunday. I felt sick and grateful for the name and address, and I buried the paper she scribbled it on in the bowels of my pocketbook. That would be tomorrow, if I couldn't find Jonathan tonight.

I would do what I had to on Sunday and take Monday off. I had two weeks of vacation due me, if I needed it. I would have to go to confession for the rest of my life.

I lock up the apartment and run down to the street. I swing down West Fourth, hear music and head toward it, flying through the traffic light, skimming between the cars, until I am halfway across the street, balanced on a strip of concrete, a median, an island. I bounce on my heels, feeling flushed.

Across the street, in the playground, a band—a guitarist, a drummer, a horn or two—is playing surrounded by a crowd. I think for a second it's Jonathan, but that second is cut short when the guitarist raises his head. He is an old man, leather-skinned, singing out in Spanish. Off to the side, a group of boys with bare, concave chests throws shots at the net-less basketball hoop. On a park bench, surrounded by friends, a girl brushes her waist-length black hair out. She counts the number of brushes aloud slowly, savoring the sound of her own voice, straining toward a hundred, as if one hundred strokes were a magical number. Her lips count eighty, eighty-one and eighty-two, and her hair shines in the ember-yellow streetlight.

I light a cigarette.

A turquoise Thunderbird drives up next to me. The car glints and glimmers. The driver whistles sharp and quick.

The cigarette burns between my teeth.

The Thunderbird revs. The driver calls out, "Come here." I don't think he is talking to me until he says it again. The light turns green and I don't cross the street. Neither, for a moment, does the Thunderbird. I grind out my cigarette with the tip of my shoe. It makes me feel sick.

And I can't stand here all night on this traffic island, with my skin glistening in the heat and car exhaust, with the pigeons like black slash marks against the blue-black sky.

The Thunderbird grows bored and speeds away.

A red rubber ball bounces into the street. From out of the music, a girl trails it across the sidewalk. She is wearing a bathing suit, black and white polka-dotted with a white frilled skirt. Her feet are wedged sandals. Her hands are outstretched. She is five or six. The ball bounces against the music, missing beats. She skips after it, crying for the ball. The music pitches louder, the crowd closing in on the band. The old man guitarist lifts his face toward the sky on a riff that never seems to end. And the ball, that red ball, skids under a battered Ford. The girl peers under the car and the ball, propelled by gravity or other forces, rolls out toward the yellow line in the street between her and me. The little girl screams. She's lost all. But this city child knows enough not to run into the street, or so I want to believe. The ball dribbles away, having its own mind. A delivery truck swerves around it. I watch the girl, watching the ball.

I shout out, "I'll get it. Stay there!"

The girl dashes off the curb between the parked cars.

"Don't!" I scream in my head before I can scream out loud, "Don't. Move."

A sudden confusion of the crowd jams the sidewalk. The Mister Softee truck rattles down the block, whirring its musical notes over and over. Nobody is listening to anybody. I imagine that I am hearing my name being called. The girl in that polka-dot bathing suit is out in the street, swinging left and right, like she doesn't know which way to go, as if any decision will be a bad one, as if stasis is better, as if her ball will roll back to her in the same way it had left her.

The light flashes yellow and red.

I hurtle into the street and back to the traffic island, displaying the ball to her, my chest hurting.

The light turns green. Traffic blows between me and the girl.

A cab honks insistently, double-parking in front of the playground. The girl looks both ways before running toward me. She grabs her rubber ball from me and secures it against her polka dots, composing herself better than I do, and stomps back across the street.

And then he steps out of the front seat of the cab.

I push the damp strands of my hair off my neck. Slowly, when the light turns green, I cross the street. I lean against the playground's fence, my shoulders pressing against the metal diamonds. His eyes flick up and down before finding mine.

He searches the concrete playground, the boys playing basketball, the girl with the hair down to her waist, and back at me, jiggling his keys.

The girl with the ball gallops toward me, pointing. Her young mother is with her. She is pretty but on the verge of fading, her teeth lapping over one another, her hair askew in a ponytail. She must have been just a child when she had her baby.

"Thank you," says the girl to me at the mother's wordless prompting. "Can I go back? Can I still play? I don't want to go to bed."

Her mother adds, "Hey, thanks a lot, from me too."

The mother swings the girl and her ball into her arms, smothers her face with kisses, and carries her back across the street, the girl's legs dangling off her hip.

"Pretty little girl," says Murray. "Good girl too. Listens to her mother." He smiles at the near memory, showing dimples.

That is when I let myself think. I give myself permission. I do it with intent. This baby could be Murray's as much as Jonathan's.

He sweats from the neck down his white shirt. He's had his hair cut off, Army regulation, or like a boy for summer. A handkerchief is rummaged out of his pocket; it needs ironing too, but is clean, and he uses it to pat down his forehead, his full lips.

"No good fares tonight," he says. "Well, one good fare out to Idlewild."

"How'd you know where to find me?"

"I called your mother."

"You did? What did she say?"

"What took me so long."

"She did not."

"She gave me your phone number and address."

"Why didn't you call?"

"What was I going to say?"

More kids surge onto the playground. The band starts up again. The mother and daughter are dancing together. The mother is swinging the little girl in and out, a kind of mambo, though the daughter wants only to jump up and down in that polka-dot bathing suit. She lets her ball roll into the corner of the fence for this moment. Then her mother swings her up into her arms. The daughter hugs herself against her mother, and the two spin and spin, and others around them clap, and they spin.

There, right there, is something I've never had with my mother: joy.

It takes me a minute to turn and face him. I must pull my eyes away from the mother and daughter.

"Makes a guy think, looking at them."

I wait to see if he is another philosopher. I don't need a philosopher. I don't need perfect pitch.

Murray shifts away. He crosses his arms, and veins run down his biceps to his hands.

"I don't know, Louise. I've got to admit, I'm a guy who spends a lot of time trying not to think about how complicated life is, and then you see something simple like this, a mother and her little girl, and I think that maybe it's not complicated. It's simple. At least for some people it's simple."

This baby can be his.

This baby inside me can be Murray's.

It rings in my ear: *This baby can be Murray's baby.*

He paces the length of the fence. He looks over at the playground. The mother hugs her daughter into her arms, and spins. "Do you want to go for a drive, Louise?" He has on the same shoes, less shine this Saturday night.

Maybe I should say no. I have the early morning appointment with the nurse. He is from nowhere, from nothing, the Bronx. I can't believe my mother just handed over my phone number and address to him.

"Let's go for a drive, okay? I can't leave the cab double-parked like this all night."

The girl with the brushed-out hair dances by herself under a string of colored lights. The music jazzes up and down the street. More people crowd into the playground. The mother and daughter leap into the center of it all, disappear.

And I climb into the front seat of his borrowed yellow cab. Murray takes us off the meter and plummets into traffic, heading east. I crank the window all the way open and let the night air in. He drives with both hands on the wheel, not too fast, not too slow. We head through the Midtown Tunnel and onto the Long Island Expressway, and after a few minutes, the road clear, we pass Maspeth.

"Where are we going?" I finally ask, breaking the silence.

"Where should we go? I just wanted to leave the city."

"The cemetery?"

"Not the cemetery."

I want to keep driving too.

•

After a half hour, we arrive at the Atlantic Ocean at Jones Beach. We park in a lot along the sand's edge, and I'm thinking that we'll talk now. He slides over and kisses my face and neck and down the scoop of my breasts.

"Murray?"

"What?" He stops with the random kisses.

I wish someone could invent a blanket that could shrink to fit into a purse for emergencies since I seem to have mine on rooftops and in cemeteries and beaches. His shoulder or elbow hits the wheel and the horn and scares the military formation of sea gulls into the night. "Let's get out of this taxi," he says.

Out of the musty stink of the cab and onto the still-warm sand, he fumbles with my bra until I reach back and unhook it. I'm not throwing this bra off a roof, or out to sea. I unbutton his plain white short-sleeved shirt and put it beneath my head. His stomach is hard and flat, matted with waves of hair. He is less cautious this time, and we make love in a hurry, clawing at one another, crabs in the sand. When we're done, he jumps up and cleans up in the ocean.

He shivers as he dunks his hands into the water and then onto his chest, willing himself still, an outline of a man at the edge of the Atlantic Ocean.

I snap myself back into my bra and pull back on my blouse. I guess I truly don't look pregnant at eight or nine weeks.

"What's next?" I ask when he returns to me. "What happens next?"

"Next?"

"My mother thought I'd never get married after I turned thirty."

"Are you thirty?" he asks.

"How old are you?"

"I'm a guy who's older than he looks, or at least that's what I've been told."

"How old?"

"You always get right to the point, Louise? I'll be thirty in August."

I say nothing. I press my hand against my stomach. This baby could his.

"So, you're thirty," he says, assuming we are the same age. "I hope to be forty someday. And eighty-seven and a hundred."

"A hundred?"

"Sure, why not?"

I touch his cheek, and he shudders. I pull back, saying to myself as much as to him, "I should finish getting dressed." I hunt for my skirt and find it half-buried in the sand. I have an unusual slowness in the core of me. Marlene will have to go with me to that nurse.

He hands me my glasses. "Don't forget these."

He breathes deep, as if needing to calm himself.

I shimmy into my skirt and curl my legs under me.

"We should go," he says. "Shouldn't we?"

"I'm actually thirty-two years old."

"Older than me," he says. "But not that old."

"I wasn't lying when I said that you were the first."

His sits down next to me and crunches his knees against his chest. Sand on his back and his hair makes him look gray and older than almost thirty. His eyes are on me, his heat, his breaths.

"Only you," I lie, hating myself a little, and then I tell him about being pregnant.

His eyes darken, comprehending what I've said. "I wore a condom."

"Army-issued from Korea. Probably Second World War vintage."

"Maybe the first, Louise," he throws back at me. "The First World War."

"Did they have condoms back then?"

A minute or two passed with silence between us, screams of an argument from the other end of the parking lot, sea gulls squawking overhead, the dull roar of the tide receding. I am ready to say I know a nurse, that I'll take care of it—but he grins. Dimples shine. "We'll get married," he says.

He's watching me, waiting.

"You go from not calling me to asking me to marry you?"

"Why not?" His big hand strokes my cheek. "I came looking for you tonight."

"Are you going to regret this someday?"

"I promise you, I'm a guy who doesn't have many regrets."

I sing in my head: *I will grow old. I will grow old with Murray.* My voice is far from perfectly pitched. He'll finish his degree. He'll teach. We'll grow old. I'll work too. I like to work. I type one hundred words a minute. I'll have to find a new job—the Army won't let me stay, married and pregnant—but I dismiss that for now. We'll have a baby. We'll grow old. He is next to me. Next to me, and he is waiting for me to say something.

"No. I'm sorry, but no," I force out.

"What?"

I shift up straight, brush the sand from my skirt, and uncurl my legs. I've lost my shoes. I can continue searching for Jonathan, or I can go to the Village nurse with Marlene, or by myself. I decide I'll go to that damn nurse by myself. I can just never go back to that playground.

My head hurts. I adjust my glasses. The ocean laps toward us, the stark smell of low tide. The sea salt curls my hair, and he wiggles his fingers into my roots. I can taste the sea on my lips, and then on his lips, which find their way back to mine. I feel light-headed and off-balance.

"I thought about you," he says after the kiss. "At all the wrong times: when I was walking to the subway, or listening to the radio, or trying to read, or in the park, shooting hoops by myself. I thought what we did—was it a dream, was it real?"

I thought how it all comes down to two people and all the unknowns.

"I love you, Murray."

"Marry me?"

I'm waiting for him to say, "I love you too." He has asked me to spend our lives together. To take his name. We are going to have a child together, maybe a little girl. We are going to have joy in our lives.

"I love you," I whisper.

"Thank you," he says.

He bends his head toward me, and I hold him in my arms.

1960

Louise was pregnant, already old, thirty-two, already written off, an excellent typist, a hundred words a minute. Her dress was sleeveless, tea-length, navy blue lace over white, with hints of lavender from the satchels in her closet. Her cat's-eye glasses were hidden in her pocket.

The ceremony was earlier at City Hall in Manhattan; no family was in attendance except Marlene, and Marlene wasn't blood.

Her mother said she would never speak to her again until there was a Roman Catholic Church wedding—with an Italian priest, not an Irish one.

The portrait was taken weeks later, at a photography studio, after she bought him a good wool suit, after she miscarried, and they decided to stay married. They would take another year to get pregnant again, and that child would be named Caroline to appease her mother. Years later, Caroline would have to make up many of these details because Murray would claim that he couldn't remember, and Louise would have lost much of her memory to an aneurysm.

Murray had to borrow his younger brother's suit for the City Hall ceremony. He told his brother, the certified public accountant, that he had an interview for a job, which he wished he did have.

He didn't tell his parents about her. They would have been angry with him in multiple languages: English, French, Russian, and most of all in Yiddish, a magnificent language to be cursed out in.

His parents owned a poultry farm in Lakewood, New Jersey and would meet her later. And to his surprise, his parents would like his bride, who knew enough to bring a gift of good French wine and to praise the chickens.

PART III

The Guest Room in Comer, Georgia

Caroline made her way in the dark to the back room, the guest room without the air conditioner. It was past midnight, and everybody else was asleep—her brother Matthew with the light on in his room, just like when he was a kid, and Pop, grumbling, restless, induced to sleep only with his pills. Her children were asleep in the wide expanse of the living room—she felt like she was putting them to sleep in a field rather than a living room. They had each kissed her and said how much fun they were having during this visit with Uncle Matthew and Grandpa Murray. She was raising polite children. She had to marvel and wonder if they were really her children, if she could be their mother. The familiar panic rising—she had grown up without a mother, now how could she be one? She wanted to crawl onto the couch with them, wrap her arms and legs around them, and make sure they knew that she was there. She wasn't leaving them. She had, however, two contrary thoughts to share with them: She wasn't going to die, and all things die. But before she could say anything, her daughter hung her arms around her neck and said they would see her in the morning while her son mumbled, half-asleep, "Night." They twisted away from her grasp and sighed into the air around her.

Earlier that day, her brother had sighed at her too. She had said to him that she refused to believe that their father was dying. There were other doctors. In New York. The best doctors.

"You can refuse it all you want," Matthew had said. "Go ahead. It won't change it."

Her daughter had asked, "Is Grandpa Murray dying?" And she couldn't say no. She waited for more questions, but her daughter just took it in and didn't ask for details. There hadn't been details. Her daughter wanted only a yes or no and sighed too.

Back in the guest room, she stood waiting for her children to cry out for her. They slept on without a sound.

After a minute of waiting, she returned to them and held her hand above their faces to make sure they were breathing, something she did even though her son was ten and her daughter four. She kissed their heads, and her daughter stirred awake at the pressure and insistence of the kisses.

It was almost midnight, and she didn't really want to wake them.

She shuffled back to the guest room. Usually the dog slept there and shed clumps of fur onto the coverlet and cotton blanket. Matthew never dusted the two oversized armoires or various dressers and tables, pieces he had collected at estate sales from local farms. He never wiped down the windows or fixed the screens. Mosquitoes and ants and flies and ticks were free to go in and out. The sheets, good sheets, Egyptian cotton, smelled of mildew and dog and sweat—her own sweat, Caroline had to think, or she couldn't sleep in this bed.

She stripped down, flung her clothes on the floor and crawled across the bed. It was too much to find her suitcase only to pull on one of her husband's old tee shirts. At her age, she should invest in a nightgown or two. She found a safe place in the center of the bed. Erik would like the size of this bed. Not that her husband would join her here, not this visit, which she decided to undertake with only a day's notice.

She spread her arms out wide like she was making angels in the snow, except it was in the middle of August, except it was stifling, except she was in this strange, oversized bed. Erik wouldn't have minded the stray fur or dust balls or buzzing of crickets or languid strands of moon and air. He wouldn't be as aware of his body as she was of hers. He preferred being naked. He'd walk around their apartment naked if she let him. He'd walk and hum. Bach or Mozart. Verdi's *La Traviata*, the opera about a prostitute, was one of his favorites. She knew he was odd, and that maybe they had been together too long.

She'd have to scold him that he couldn't be naked. The children could walk in on them, though they had never done so. He couldn't be bold and naked when she wanted to hide her body.

Her father never seemed to forget about his children in the way her husband often seemed surprised to see two representatives of his gene pool running through their apartment. It was a good thing that he wasn't here with her.

She ran one leg up the other leg. She felt her stretch marks, the scars that wouldn't fade, the heat and roundness of her belly. She should get up and check again on her children. When she propped herself up, she felt dizzy, bereft, a bit sick. She laid back down again, lumbering to her side, her breasts heavier than usual, aching, wanting to be held in place. She should start wearing a sports bra to bed. A nightgown and bra and socks. Ever since college, her husband had joked that her feet were cold and that's why she loved him—his were warm.

He had asked her to join him in west Texas on his research trip, and she refused. She had work as well. She couldn't go watch her husband work. Yet when her brother called her, she had taken off from her job for a week and had driven straight down here. Her husband hadn't said anything to her about her change in plans. She turned on her stomach, mashed her face into the muck of the down feather pillow.

If her husband were here, he'd tell her again that they should buy a bed this size for their small Manhattan apartment. He'd look out the window for moths. He'd loved watching the moon and stars in this sky void of any light pollution. He'd be comfortable in a way she could never be in this bed.

She tossed. A lepidopterist. Her Pop knew what that was from the first time she said, "Erik is studying to be a lepidopterist," though his first response was "Bet you can't say that ten times fast. So, he's the man? He's going to study butterflies? They pay you for that?"

She flipped on her back, steadied her breasts, held them in her hands, squeezed, clamped down her sadness. Imagined Erik, her lepidopterist—she couldn't say it fast—imagined his hands, his teeth, his tongue, ached for him and said, "Fuck you," out loud.

She could survive without her husband for a night, or a week, or even until the end of August when he was due back in Manhattan from the Texas hills. She had spoken with him briefly today. Had told him that her father was in bad shape, a shell of himself, with the Parkinson's and lymphoma and deluge of medicines and doctors.

"Erik, your kids miss you," she said in even tones. She wanted to make sure that he knew this call was about him too, not just about her or her father.

Erik said nothing until he said, "The winds are rising, the butterflies are mating," and then they lost their signal, and she couldn't get it back, couldn't call from Comer to somewhere in the Texas hills.

She slept, restless, for a while, until she woke all at once. Lost. Her head was muddled with her nightmare, another trip down the endless hallways—sometimes they were the hospital halls, sometimes they were darker, more medieval, confused, like tonight. She had to break the pitch-black silence. She reached for her phone. Checked her messages. None from him.

She waited to hear the dog bark. She was sure that someone's name was being called. Not hers. Not "Caroline." No one was calling for her, or her other name, for "Mommy."

A hot wind pushed through the curtains. Her breasts swayed, blue-veined. Her bones felt sore, as if more time had passed than just one or two hours since she put her children to bed.

Right outside her window, pickups raced down the road, one or two backfiring; a brood of owls hooted, amplified by the darkness; the dog, finally, whimpered and barked. Pop shouted out against his ghosts. He roughed out her mother's name, "Louise!"

She felt like she'd been punched.

"Louise!"

She fought to swallow, her throat tight and dry, and she clasped her arms around herself. She should go see if her father was okay.

Mosquitoes swam through the tiny breaks in the screens, buzzing unseen. They stung the back of her legs. She slapped at them, furiously hitting herself, missing them. Erik had once told her only female mosquitoes bite, as if that explained something. If she let him, he would have gone into detail. She always used to love how he explained things at length to the kids, read them books, worked on their homework with them, watched television shows on Animal Planet, from kittens to parasites, for hours. He researched monarch butterflies. Since the beginning of May, he had been in west Texas for their last mating season of the year, the butterflies, the monarchs.

Sweat dripped down between her breasts. The bites itched and swelled with a vengeance. She was sleep-deprived, tattooed with stretch marks and birthing scars, cast out. She'd go to her Pop. Go to her children. Make sure they were all still there.

She stumbled out of bed and yanked at the white sheet, draping it down on her shoulders. Wrapping the sheet around her, she took a step toward the door. And Erik shambled into her brother's spare room.

He tossed his backpack off his shoulder onto the disarray of bedding. He had on jeans and a concert tee shirt from the Met Opera in Central Park. He looked like he could be twenty-two again, except the blond hair was thinning, receding, revealing the strong, sunburned lines of his forehead and skull. She thought she'd see the moon, but no moon had followed him here. He was humming too, humming one last low bass note, breathing through his aquiline nose, and she imagined that he saw a younger version, also twenty-two, at least for a moment.

"Why?" she asked. "Why are you here?"

And he looked like he might take the time to explain.

"No, tell me in the morning," she said. "I need to sleep."

His fingers slipped inside the sheet. "The butterflies mated," he said. "A kaleidoscope of orange and yellow and black."

She let him tease the sheet up over her head and heard the thrum of his heart, felt the dry, measured breaths on her face. A sigh.

"Did you know that monarchs' copulating can last up to sixteen hours?" he started to say.

She raced to his mouth and covered his with hers. He bent his knees at the force of her and scooped her up, the sheet fluttering.

Morning in Comer

Nobody is getting a decent bagel. If you want lox, the only option is seal-wrapped in plastic and labeled 'smoked salmon.' You can't get lox carved so thin it lays on your tongue, tasting of salt and sea. If you want tongue, old-fashioned pickled beef tongue, you can't get tongue either. But then you could hardly find that back in New York so easy, and I can live without tongue. Still, don't bother with trying to order a pastrami sandwich around here; they'll sell you barbecue. It will be *trayf*, not kosher by any means, but pretty good if you want barbecue and not a pastrami sandwich on rye with a sour pickle wedged next to it on the plate. You can't get any appetizings around here: whitefish or chopped herring or herring in sour cream with raw onions that stay on your breath until the end of the day. No chopped liver. You can't even say something isn't chopped liver. Either way people will look at you funny. Anyway, here they only know appetizers, and they are before meals. Where I'm from, appetizing is the meal. And you can't get it here. Blintzes and latkes can't be bought, and somehow, if you try to make them from scratch, they don't taste the same no matter how many potatoes you peel or how much *schmalz* you use. I wouldn't even know where to start to make a *knish* or *kishka* or *kasha varnishkes*. I don't think they sell what they're made of down here. The ingredients come from small factories in Brooklyn with names like Acme, where you'd think they sell spare parts or scrap metal. For dessert, don't expect a spread of *babka* or *rugelach* or *hamentashen*. The triangle symbolized the evil king, my mother would tell me every year.

"What evil king?" I once asked at eight or nine years old.

"Any evil king. All of them. Eat."

My memories are out of order. I'm sitting here in my son's kitchen waiting for lunch or dinner, or something else, wanting to remember what's important. I'm not hungry. I haven't been hungry in a long time. Besides, Matthew likes to feed me what he thinks is good for me. Kale. Who ever heard of kale?

I just had a nice talk with my son-in-law. Caroline's husband. He appeared out of nowhere and made me a cup of tea. I apologized that we didn't have any decent bagels. He proceeded to go in detail about why the bagels in Manhattan, where he lives, are different. It's the water; everybody knows that. He went on for about ten minutes about the reservoir and the water tunnels and copper pipes before he wrapped up, and I could go back to dreaming of a perfectly round and fresh-from-the-oven New York bagel, a plain bagel, the beginning and end of life in a bagel like that.

That son-in-law is off now in the garden with his and Caroline's children, wanting to pick out something green, he said, for breakfast. I don't know what green things anyone eats for breakfast. I hope it's not kale.

If I were making this meal, I'd make it lunch and start with a nice matzo ball soup. The matzo balls would be fluffed and light, a little seltzer does the trick, the soup not too salty, the noodles slippery, savory. I'd tell the old joke—it was old when it was new: *A diner sees a fly in his soup. 'What's that fly doing in the soup?' he asks the waiter. The waiter glances down. 'The backstroke.'*

If I were getting the food ready for the family, I'd have bowls of fruit too. Bananas. Oranges. Pomegranates, full of seeds, the fruit of beginnings. The juice would stain hands and lips. The kids would crack up and spit the seeds at one another. I'd stick a wedge in my mouth and make funny faces.

And the blueberries. On the chicken farm, my mother prepared for me bowls of blueberries with sour cream and sugar. Or did I feed that to the kids?

"Get outside. Get those blueberries before the birds eat them all up. And I don't want to see any green ones. Pick the big, ripe blue ones!" Am I screaming because I'm angry? I'm not. The kids should know that food can be gathered from trees and bushes and dug from the ground. Food can be foraged, or stolen, if it must be.

I fed the kids the best deli I could afford. Feasts. I fed them feasts, and I'd do it again if I could find anything worth eating around here.

And remember that Coleman stove? The camping trips to Cranberry Lake? I'd make big pots of oatmeal—thick and warm with milk and honey and raisins. Get the kids up at dawn for that oatmeal. Somehow it was even better, even sweeter with the sun rising on the lake. I brought the kids camping every year. Must be thirty years old, that Coleman stove. I tested it before packing it into the minivan when I left Florida for what I thought would be a short visit to Comer, and that stove flared right up, hot and even flames. When I'm feeling better, and ready to leave Comer, I should remember that stove.

What I miss the most is bread. Man can live without a warm place to sleep, without a bath, without an embrace or a kind word but not without bread. In the last few months here, I've worked at baking my own, kneading the dough, letting the yeast rise —a rye bread with seeds, a rye without, once even a *challah* on a Friday, which turned out as heavy as a baby. Matthew liked that bread too. But my hands don't work right anymore. And Matthew won't let me use the new stove, not after a mishap with the timer and a loaf of pumpernickel, which nearly burned down the whole place.

Even so, nothing smells like it used to. Nothing tastes like it used to either, especially the bread. Matthew says it's the Parkinson's affecting my senses; it's the neural transmitters out of whack, breaking down. It's not the lack of brisket and rye with seeds. It's the Parkinson's, and not, what I think, the loneliness or yearning for what once nourished me. I never thought I'd wish for hunger. Still I yearn for my appetite to return, for a *bisele* of hunger, and to find solace once more in the symbol of the completeness of life, a decent New York bagel.

Willie and Pop

This Thursday night in early October, with the first scent of a raw winter coming, the hardening of the red-clay earth wracked with drought, and the winter vegetables, the squash and onions and pumpkins, lined up on the long cook's countertop, Matthew wants out. Out here in the Georgia countryside, he hasn't seen a soul but me in a week; he hasn't been out without me in a month. He needs a night, and I say, "Go."

"I'll be back late, Pop. Don't wait up," Matthew says to the dog and me. Then, hesitating at the back door, he asks, "You have your cell phone on you? I charged it, didn't I?"

"Go," I say. I have no clue where that damn phone is. "Enjoy the dinner. Where you off to again?"

"I told you," he says. "That new steak place in Athens."

"I like steak."

Matthew settles back those big shoulders of his, runs his hand through the shorn hair, a buzz cut. He's a bulkier, muscular version of my younger self. He could be me at forty years old. He's a good-looking guy, my son. But he isn't going to take me along tonight no matter what I say. I can tell his mind is made up.

"Bring us home the leftovers," I say. His black Labrador, Willie, lies next to my chair and flags his tail from one side to the other.

"You have your phone on you, Pop? If I call you, answer it."

"Got it right here." I press my hands to my flannel bathrobe. "Don't worry. Go already. Worst thing in the world is to keep friends waiting to eat."

"Willie, watch out for Pop, okay?" he says, caring as much about the dog as he does me. He pets the dog.

"Go." I add under my breath, "I don't need anybody looking out for me," but he's already out the door.

•

With Matthew gone, Willie scratches and licks his ass. His fur shines bare in spots, his eyesight poor, one eye clouded so it always looks like twilight, his back legs arthritic and achy, especially in the early morning or late at night. He sniffs at the old man, who is rising from his chair. He stretches his front paws out and clomps after him to the kitchen.

Around the old man is always food—either accidently dropped to the ground or snuck to him under the table. Matthew doesn't like the old man feeding him from his plate. Willie eats what is offered, makes the old man happy.

But tonight there is only more dog food in his dish.

Willie worries the old man is growing bone-thin while he, the dog, gets fatter and slower and forgets to go outside to pee. Willie tries not to forget and is proud that tonight he whimpers to be let out into the cool night air, and after a minute or two, the old man makes his way over and bangs the door wide open.

The sky is filled with the moon and the smell of wood burning beyond the pine trees. He lifts his leg over the rosebushes, now without flowers. He lingers along the edge of the porch, barks at a deer or two, and yearns to be once again a dog that bounds over the fields and chases deer under the glittering stars. Instead, he turns around to check that the old man is still there. The old man has left the door open, and he is shuffling along the porch in his slippers. The dog glances at the fields and woods one last time, his snout caressing the night air, until he reminds himself that his job was to watch over the old man.

•

After a few moments of standing with the dog in the moonlight, Willie raising his snout to the stars as if he could smell their lights, me wishing that I had learned the constellations, which stars were planets, thinking that once I get back home to Florida, I'm going to buy a telescope at the flea market, I urge the dog back into the house.

"You ready, Willie? You going to stay here in Georgia with Matthew or come to Florida with me? Maybe I should pee first too."

I hit it off the porch.

The dog labors back toward me. "I don't think you're going to last the winter, Willie. What is Matthew going to do without you?" I scratch behind his ears and then mine. I need a haircut. The dog's fur is mangy, moist. We both stink from pee. I struggle to tie closed my robe, and then, because the fingers don't work right anymore, just leave it open. There's nobody around to care.

Back in the house with the dog, I also leave the door slightly ajar. I realize this when I am already across the other side of the kitchen. "Matthew will lock up when he comes back, when he finishes up that fancy steak. Probably costing a small fortune for that dinner, Willie."

I take in the expanse of his kitchen, the granite countertops, the stainless-steel appliances, including the new professional cook stove, a small fortune.

The dog barks.

But then that dog barks at everything: shadows, the lights from the pickups speeding down the road, the high winds off the foothills. I sway, and I grip granite counter. "How about some popcorn?" I ask the dog, who barks what I am sure is a yes.

Soon enough the bag explodes in that microwave of Matthew's and the kitchen tingles with a warm, buttery smell. If I could still dance, I would at that popcorn smell, the aroma of long-ago movie nights. I don't bother pouring it into a bowl, something Matthew would make me do. I scuff along until I locate the remote for the television and lower myself into my chair. I don't bother to turn on a light. Matthew is always leaving all the lights on in this big house, scared I'll fall, he says. I don't need the lights. Just like I don't need steak. I can take care of myself.

•

Willie sticks his nose into his bowl, into his dog food, and sloughs through a bite or two of the organic turkey gourmet cobbler dog food for older dogs. He'd rather have steak. He laps up some water and pads over to the old man, circling him, making sure everything is in order. With a sigh, he lies down next to him. He is rewarded with a rough pat on the head and a handful of popcorn.

Willie munches on the popcorn and reviews his life again. He has the old man and Matthew. He has the warm farmhouse and the run of the fields. He has as much as he wants to eat. He has the life for a big, ugly mutt, even if at times he wouldn't have minded a bitch for long nights like this one.

"I think I'll go tomorrow, Willie," says the old man. "Just have to load up the van with my stuff and I'm out of here. What you say? Good idea?"

Willie nudges his wet nose between the old man's swollen legs, another pat, another handful of popcorn, and another very long night.

•

Usually, I follow the subtitles to keep my mind sharp. This night I know the black-and-white World War II movie so well I can recite the dialogue: "*Of all the gin joints in all the towns in all the world....*" Instead, I doze through the scenes at Rick's. I perk up when Laszlo sticks it to the Nazis and gets the crowd at Rick's to stand and sing the *Marseillaise* with the Nazis brass right there. Of course, the band strikes up only after Rick—Humphrey Bogart—nods for them to play. Rick is in love with Ilsa—Ingrid Bergman. So am I. But Rick and Ilsa will always have Paris, and I'm here dreaming of women. I miss the women. Once I believed that as I got older, I'd think less of them, less of sex, but I think of it more, and more often of Louise.

I can't understand how Matthew likes other men when there are such women walking the earth. But who am I to judge? He's a good boy even if he didn't bring his father out for a steak dinner. I just have to get myself out from Georgia and back to Florida. He's taken away my car and my driver's license. Who's he kidding? I can still drive.

I look up at the TV. There's that actress there who I always liked. I always liked smart women, wisecracking, funny women. And tall women too. Or did I like short? No, I am sure I admired them statuesque. She is smoking a cigarette through darkened lip buds. I sniff the air as if I can smell her smoke or perfume. I close my eyes, only for a minute or two.

The dog rustles at my feet. A scratching step, a squeaking sound, a scratching trail against the kitchen floor—and we both tense, awake. The air in the house has changed, become colder. No lights flick on. "Quiet down," I say to the dog, who's crouching down at my side. "Matthew, that you?"

The dog growls toward the other side of the long open room, toward the kitchen. "Sit. I'll go see what's going on." I struggle to my feet and press forward. From off the wall, I grab a broom with a thick wooden handle and a wide base, a useless broom, handmade and designed for show, scented with of all things, cinnamon.

Something clatters and scratches across the floor. The dog barks sharp and loud. "Good dog," I say. "What do you see?" I don't see anything.

The dog circles around me, barking. The dumb animal, I nearly trip over him. I shake the broom at the dog to get him out of my way.

I drag myself across the wide-open space between the television and the kitchen. I ask myself, not for the first time, how the hell did I end up in Georgia? On the whole there are good people in Comer, except for the kids in the trailer down by the river growing marijuana and mixing chemicals for what they call meth. But if anyone is breaking into this house, I am going to crack his skull open with this broom. I am going to show him that I am still a guy from the Bronx.

I will my feet toward the open screen door. The legs don't want to move as fast as the brain wants them to go. I've felt more disconnected from my body since I've come here, as if I left a younger self in Florida. "I have an eighteen-year-old mind in an eighty-two-year old body" is what I've started saying to Matthew. The kid nods, not agreeing or disagreeing, but looking tired and sad. Who's going to take care of him when I'm gone? When he's old? I make a mental note: I'm going to bring this up to Matthew in the morning.

The dog barks, and I remember the broom in my hand and the open door.

I take a step and raise the broom as high as I can. My hands and shoulders shake with the effort.

Eyes glow yellow in the dark toward me. A dank smell wafts across the kitchen. A hiss. The dog growls.

"Get the hell out of here." I bash the broom down near the dog's food dish, onto the back of the intruder. A raccoon. The mind is sharp; the blow fumbles. Fur bristles. I stand between the raccoon and the dog. I don't want the dog to get hurt.

"Out!" I lower the broom again, swatting the raccoon in the face. The animal rears up but doesn't run. Might be hungry or rabid or both.

I work hard to catch my breath, stumbling, staggering with the broom, feeling the cold from the open door at my back, knowing if I scream there isn't a neighbor within a mile, only those long-haired boys down by the river in their trailer.

The raccoon springs. The dog lunges from behind me, baring his teeth.

•

Willie attacks that raccoon the moment it goes for the old man. He wrestles with the black and gray fur and snags the raccoon by the neck, by the vein that pulses back to its heart. He tastes blood. Smells meat and woods and acorns on his enemy, smells that incite even an old dog like him and make him feel young.

The old man teeters against Matthew's kitchen workstation. A pumpkin rolls from the countertop to the floor and splits open. White seeds spill out.

He shakes the raccoon in his teeth, aiming to break its neck.

The raccoon hisses, a terrible seething from the back of its throat, and sets his steel-sharp nails on him. Willie fights on. He whips the raccoon across the kitchen floor and leaps on it again, tearing at the raccoon's neck, tufts of fur tumbling like desiccated grasses across Matthew's polished kitchen floor.

"Get him, Willie," he hears the old man urging him on, but he doesn't need encouragement. Willie has instinct and bears down, even though he is scraped and bloodied and wounded.

The old man rises the broom to strike. "Good boy," he says. "Let me at him."

Willie fights on, his jaws clamped down on the other animal's spine. The old man lowers the broom, and he trips. He comes down to the floor, eye to eye with him, at the same moment.

Willie's jaw crushes down, breaks through raccoon bone. Fur and flesh obscure his sight. The taste of warm blood slides down his throat and the scent of fresh meat inflames him. He snarls and pounces and drops the dead raccoon in front of Matthew's new stove. He flings back his snout and howls, a keening into the night, reaped from the depths where he is still as much wolf as dog.

•

I lie on the kitchen floor in acute, spiking pain.

I try to reach for my cell phone in my pocket where it should be, but isn't. I attempt to drag my legs close to me. Across the room, the movie is rolling its long list of credits. The Nazis are defeated once again. I pant and the dog pants next to me. His fur is torn.

From somewhere in the house, that damn cell phone rings. And rings.

I hope Matthew is enjoying that steak dinner.

Blood seeps down the side of my face onto the shirtsleeve of my flannel robe. I've been here in Comer for how long? A year already? Matthew helps me button up my pants and shirts even when I tell him no. He takes me to doctors and doles out the pills even when I tell him that I've had enough. I wonder if he does it all because he loves his old man, or because I showed up at his doorstep and collapsed, and that was that. My daughters have families, my youngest son has a family. Matthew only has me.

I'm going to pack up and go as soon as I can. He needs his own family too.

My legs jerk. I must stand up. I don't want Matthew to find me on the floor and ruin his night. Willie paces around me, his dog breath against my cheek. I want to reach out to pet him, to reassure him, but my arms have lost their will. Instead, the dog licks my hands and raises his gristly snout to test the air around my head. I'm cold. I close my eyes. I am seeing blue-white sky when it should be night. I love him, my eldest son, and I'm sure I've never told him that in so many words: *I love you.*

•

Willie howls. The old man doesn't move. He sniffs the air. The smells are all wrong: pumpkin, fur, mud, animal blood, human blood.

I Had a Mother

I said I had a mother.

My mother—I practiced saying that.

My younger brothers and sister never claim out loud that I was their mother. The curse on my head was to be sister and mother to them and to fail at both. (I'm sorry, brothers. I'm sorry, sister).

I couldn't be my own mother.

I played at being casual talking about my mother, grouping my father and mother in their unit of 'parents.' I often stumbled and had to pick 'parents' off my tongue, staying with father and mother.

I had a mother; truly, I had her only for a blink, birth and a few years after that. A blood vessel broke. I found her on the bathroom floor when I was four and a half. What I said to my siblings: "Mommy hit her head; she'll be back soon." What children ever think that their mother has a life without them? After the first stroke, my mother lived on in wheelchairs and side-up nursing home beds. When my Pop divorced her, I was twenty-two, and designated her legal next of kin.

I had a mother, of course I did. Everyone does. I should be able to tell the story of a motherless child, but that would involve laying bare what happened over all those years—a struggle with being responsible for her, instead of her for me. An admittance: my young sister was a more devoted daughter than me. So I shrug and say, "You see, my mother…," as if preparing a longer story, as if I knew her story, and my breath catches hard in my chest.

The death certificate stated congestive heart failure. I said I had a mother and this proved it. She was buried, and taps was played on the sliver of a cemetery hill for her. A pair of soldiers in dress uniforms presented a flag to me in a tight triangle. I had a mother, and she once served in the Army, before I was born. I should have claimed that too. Cold rain with the promise of snow and the scent of ozone cut the air thin.

The grave had to be opened by hand. The gravediggers, in rolled-up shirtsleeves, stood only slightly to the side, leaning on their shovels. They'd place her casket on top of the casket of my grandmother, who was buried on top of my grandfather. "Three in a grave," said the boss of the gravediggers. "They don't make them like that anymore. Used to be for parents to be buried with an infant child." He glanced sideways at me. His mouth rearranged into a smile of missing teeth.

I said I felt like I was burying my own child.

I am so proud.

I had a mother, you see.

Comer

Comer is seventeen miles from Athens on a two-lane highway where the ever-present 'Buckle Up It's The Law' signs are designed to look like the Confederate flag.

My brother moved there from Atlanta in 2005

I've driven eighteen hours from Manhattan over two days, and I only want to go home. Matthew has renovated a former factory on ten acres of land, which he calls 'Flower Hill' and everyone in Comer calls 'the sock factory' because it used to be the factory that made men's dress and athletic socks.

My father collapsed in Comer in 2006

Pop, who's survived hypothermia and the Korean War, lymphoma and prostate cancer, now has congestive heart disease along with Parkinson's. The doctor in Athens tells us he has six months to live. He calls both his girlfriends in Coconut Creek with the news that he's not coming back for a while.

Four and a half years pass in Comer

Matthew must sell Pop's condo in Florida. I visit Comer three or four times a year over the next few years. One autumn, I come to know Miss Martha, who makes fig jam. I buy all of her two dozen jars at the weekly farmer's market, and she says, "Bless your heart, you're Murray's daughter. He has a sweet tooth too." She swaddles newspapers around each jar for the trip to New York, as if reluctant to give them up to me. "I can't imagine who is going to eat all this jam," and I don't want to tell her that I am going to eat all the seed-full fig jam and think of her with her sunspots and floppy straw hat and pink frosty lipstick with fondness. Pop's dimples flash at Miss Martha, even as his legs forget how to move. Later Matthew tells me that Pop has asked Miss Martha out, and she refused him, saying that she had never met a Jew before him, and while he sure is a cute one, she's a God-fearing woman. I want to tell her that I fear God too, but instead Pop buys more fig jam from her and mails it to me.

All-American 4th of July in Comer

A band concert and fireworks at night in Athens, and a daytime fair in Comer before then—boiled peanuts, pies, and sweet tea. Local peach or praline ice cream. County fire trucks parked out for the kids, and towards the back, a flea market. Our family loves flea markets as much as other families love football, and we hurry toward those tables. In the last row, Confederate memorabilia is for sale. Swastikas on armbands and flags—some real antiques, we are informed—are for sale. KKK pamphlets, take one. We turn and leave the 4th of July fair.

It's only target practice

Matthew has built us all a long back porch by hand since he says he can't do his art while he's taking care of Pop. The two men have planted rose bushes and grapevines all along the porch, which overlooks several acres of red-clayed fields. Pop has hung hummingbird feeders, and there are a dozen that visit with him, whirring in the air. Pop muses about making wine, about travelling to me in New

York. He says he has a lot of things he still wants to do. He confides that he's afraid that my brother is lonely, even with him visiting here. "You live here, you're not visiting," says Matthew, exhausted. Pop shakes his head at this idea. He gossips that the closest neighbor, on the other side of the wood, has four generations living on their property. If I'm having trouble with my husband, we could move down here for a while too, he says. I want to ask if the neighbors buckle up. The last night of our trip, our three generations sit outside in the cool night air. My father and brother have bought my kids a top-of-the-line telescope, and they are actually taking turns spotting constellations. Across the fields, a sharp ping cuts through the quiet of the stars. Matthew says, "It's only the neighbors at target practice." *Ping. Ping.* "Maybe they see some deer," Pop says. *Ping. PING.* I shout for the kids. The neighbors are shooting at us.

2012. My father is finally dying, sort of

It's the third week of August, and my father's eighty-second birthday, the fifth he'd celebrate in Comer. He now has a wheelchair and a hospital bed. A nurse visits from the Veteran's Administration twice a week. I drive straight down from New York without my husband. The radio is broken. The air conditioning is fussy. My son and daughter are worse than fussy, fighting in the back seat. I make my daughter play music on her iPod to distract me, and them. For hours One Direction beats over us as hot air and bugs rush through the open windows. My brother says he wants to bury Pop in Comer, when it's time. I say, "Absolutely not. Never. Not over my dead body," and we laugh at this until our hearts hurt. The kids don't understand why we are laughing and race around us until they fall at our feet. "I'm living to a hundred," interjects Pop. I tell my brother that I can't make one more trip to Comer.

October

My brother is the brave one. He's with Pop when the heart goes, when the stroke hits. The body is flown back to New York and is buried in a cemetery in Long Island, near his mother and father. Years before, my mother was buried with her parents in a Catholic cemetery, another tale of divide. My brother sells his place in Comer and moves north. He starts to paint birds; some are hummingbirds, a thing he never did before. Every fall, to my surprise, I miss the taste of Miss Martha's fig jam.

Last Chance

Hell is cold. Don't listen to the Italians, or to those who imagine the fire and brimstone and all that. Hell is cold inside your bones. And then, it's the cold steaming to the surface. First your fingertips go violet and you have to check that they're still attached to your hands, or your toes to your feet. Cold is the stone weight of your breath inside your chest. I've had blood transfusions and for the briefest of moments could feel the surge of warmth, which was almost worse than always being cold; other people's blood, breadcrumbs to a hungry man, a girl's peck on the cheek to an ugly one. Not that I'm hungry or ugly.

I have lugged a folding chair out into the unrelenting Georgia sun and planted it around that yard as if I were the sundial and the light and warmth spilling from the noontime sun could heal me, or better yet, turn back time on me, and still I was cold. I hope none of the kids will ever be cold like that. At the end, I had an eighteen-year-old mind in an eighty-two-year-old body. That body is in the ground now. Hell is cold, and I have every reason to believe in Hell, in payback, in retribution, but for the first time in a long time, I'm not cold.

I'm just a guy from the Bronx. At the end of the day that's how I like to think of myself. That's how Louise truly knew me. Nice Roman Catholic girl from Maspeth in Queens, New York. Louise would call this Heaven. Lavender, grasses, earth—that was always her scent. I have dreamed of her in all my dreams, and maybe that's all that this is. I am dead, and this is my punishment—to drift in her scent.

I don't think I can do it.

Louise.

I see now. The kids have left cuttings on the grave, purples and reds, lavender and roses, as if they couldn't make up their minds. I always wanted to be buried right into the ground. Let the earth take me back. But Caroline insisted on spending money, and they were ripped off by that *gonif* funeral director. I still think in the old words. Louise used to tease me that I couldn't be angry or in love in English, only in Yiddish.

What can I say now? The kids should have dug me into my son's vegetable garden in Comer, in Georgia. At least there, I'd be among the tomatoes as big as my hand, bursting ripe. But my body was flown back to New York after all these years, not to the cemetery with the cupids and crucifixes on the hill, not there, not next to Louise. That would be against somebody's goddamned rules. I am buried in a Jewish cemetery out on Long Island, near my father and mother.

Truth be told, I am relieved to give up my broken-down bones. I stayed almost too long in Comer. I never wanted to outstay any welcome.

Even so, I have to ask forgiveness of only one person. Louise. That's it. Maybe that's why I'm here instead of at peace in the grave. Or maybe Jews, alive or dead, wander.

Louise—

My voice echoes back to me. Riding the air with it is the smell of dying roses in October—the buds bent, the petals gone, the scent from deep within the flower. Thing is I don't know if the smell is real, if I'm coming or going, if this is hello or goodbye.

I kept my word to Louise. My first and last thoughts of every day were about the kids. The kids without a mother, kids with me for their Pop, even if none of them are kids anymore.

Forgive me for all I said and all I didn't say.

I'm the guy who ran even if I stayed. I'm the guy who hid in plain sight. Forgive me. Absolve me of the past, of memory, of scenes that were mine and feel like they should have been someone else's, playing in black and white, playing in a loop in my head, filming without film.

If this is Heaven, shouldn't there be angels? Shouldn't there be others? The quiet roars across rising winds. I am going at an easy gait, the strength back in my legs.

Louise?

I should go. I should leave. I have stayed too long in one place.

Maybe this is Hell, or I am in the cold wet earth, winter coming soon, and there is no Heaven or Hell. It's all crazy. But if Louise is out there in the vastness of this universe: Murray Blech has died.

Louise!

Something lifts in me, or maybe a breeze or wind whispers at me, and I am loose and light-footed, and so I call out her name, as if not trusting myself. "Louise? Are you here?"

"Murray?" she throws back at me, airily.

There's no going to her. She's with me. "Louise, do you forgive me?"

"For what?"

"For what? Let's start with that hospital."

"Hudson River State Psychiatric Center."

"The moans, the smells of urine and sweat and rotten eggs and the attempt of bleach to cover it all up, the moans in the lobby, in the hallways, from every room, the suffering, the moans. And I abandoned you there, left you as a ward of the state. How does one ask forgiveness?"

"What else?"

"What else?" I repeat, annoyed at her lack of gravity for the situation.

"I'm far from there now. Go on. What else?"

"Okay, give me a minute. I forgot all the kids' birthdays, all of them. And I left them alone once or twice for a night or two, or for an entire weekend. I had a few girlfriends, maybe more than a few."

"Nobody expected you to be an angel."

"I got sick. The kids had to take care of me, or at least Matthew did, and his dog."

The clouds part, and I can see the four of them near the grave, the four kids huddled close after the service.

"Murray."

"Worst thing, and I should have said this first. I never talked much about you, Louise, not to the kids."

She sighs, and I remember that impatient sigh all too well—it's all about exasperation with me, my failings.

"Louise?" I say, wanting to make sure she is still there, wanting to say her name, to pull her close. I don't know where I am, only somewhere inky dark. "What else do you need to know?"

I strain to hear her in the thunderous, deafening, frightening silence.

"You're asking me?" she says out of the dark.

"Who else?"

My thoughts shift away from me. A breeze, a scent of fresh earth, of spring plants in the ground.

"Louise, other men made names for themselves." I shiver. "Let's face it, what did I do?"

I can sense a river receding, a wind going out to sea. I want to follow her, feel her weight and length against me.

"What's that sound?" I ask her.

"You know what it is." She is leaving me.

I keep talking, desperate for her to stay near. "I thought it was the beating of my heart, but it can't be, can it?" I grin at my heart's stubborn pretense.

"The kids are laughing."

"At what?" I strain to hear the chatter at my grave. I want to go, to escape into the nothingness that seems to await me, but I stay. "What are they laughing at?"

"They're telling one another stories, talking about their Pop."

Through the blackness, I hear it too, and something else. Louise is humming, hitting the notes for the first time in her life, as far as I can tell. The last dance from that night at the Palladium. Her sounds ripple the air around us, leading me toward her.
Imagine her hips swaying in that red dress with the slipping shoulder strap, and me dancing with her. Imagine the taste of her mouth— stained with tobacco and a trace of rum and Coke.

"Remember that song? The Drifters."

"Do you forgive me?" I have to ask one more time. If light shines, I don't need light; if air surrounds me, I don't need air, but I need this. I'm making my final pitch, like I'm going to be thrown out, shown the door.

"There's nothing to forgive. Come home."

A brush of something warm, silk or skin, draws me even nearer, and music, a saxophonist, or a trumpet. Her arms wrap around me, strong arms. The scent of lavender encircles us, as if from a great field.

"Hello, Murray."

And so, we dance, on the two.

PART IV

Temerarious:

marked by temerity: rashly or presumptuously daring
—*Merriam-Webster Dictionary*

We live in the glass house across from the park. We have a temerarious love—you want to live in a house with walls, but we've stayed together. Until one moonless night, we threaten to call in the lawyers—your brother, my cousin—and make a pretense that we will be calm, temperate, mollified. Our story has no dénouement, nothing after the climax, only the climax, physical and metaphysical, though you argue: "What use are stories?" Books are the first thing dictators destroy, poets are the first murdered. Where else can we find truth? "Not in books." I cannot live without books—they are piled about our bed; they are queued in my devices as well as my heart. You turn on cable news. Evenings of silence follow in our glass house. And then one day, before the dog walkers and senior striders occupy the park, early morning wordless sex—sex for relief of our individual nightmares, for the stories we won't tell one another, sex on bindings knocked to the floor, on a novel by, on a short story collection of, on the complete works of poetry for. Afterwards the air is swollen and fetid and unsustainable with what's between us until you ask: "How does this end?" Rashly, presumptuously daring, I think: *This is why I love you. You want me to write our story.*

Perseids

"But the stars that marked our starting fall away. We must go deeper into greater pain, for it is not permitted that we stay."

– *The Divine Comedy* by Dante Alighieri

The heat does not break but I demand the windows wide open. Even more: I plan to stay up and see the shower of meteors at the sky's perimeter, and my lover demands the windows shut. He's going to sleep, and all the Perseids in the universe won't stop him. Once when I was twelve or thirteen, my Pop didn't even notice that I left the house. I roamed The Hill by the schoolyard with the first who would ever kiss me. We lost count of the falling stars. We discovered that we didn't know where the curve of the sky began or ended, only that it led to trails of light. We kissed. I'd leave my Pop's chaotic house many more times until at seventeen I left for good. *Peripatetic* describes me—itinerant, travelling, roving, unsettled. Tonight, my lover seals off the summer's heat; a proper blanket is procured. He prepares to sleep, not make love, not to go into the night, "not to see rocks, that's all they are, call them what you want: meteors; they aren't stars." He topples into the cooled somnolence without even a kiss. And on this last moonrise of August, on an anniversary of sorts—the night my father was born, the night I was first kissed—are there other excuses I can conjure? It is not permitted that I stay. I miss my Pop with an even deeper pain than I thought I would. I wander into a shattering of darkness. This is not a dream—the stars fall around me and the trees are all on fire. I pick up stars, fill my pockets, and go where the sky leads me.

A Kholem: A Dream

Grandmother Rose and her older sisters, the ones who played the violin, chatter like the birds. My grandmother is bringing them to see me, these two sisters who never had children. "English. She only speaks English," she admonishes them with a certain pride in the only language she and I shared. She had trained as a dressmaker with her sisters in Paris, where she developed a taste for wine that wasn't blood-thick and kosher. After she sailed to America to reunite with my grandfather, she sent letters to her sisters urging them to immigrate too, but they had their elderly parents and had returned to Warsaw—*well,* the sisters wrote, *someone had to stay behind.* The Nazis murdered them all. My grandmother and her sisters float over my head, a Chagall in motion. They call me *Chaya*: Caroline. They stroke my hair and face, kiss my cheeks—*Kinderlach:* dear child. *Shayna maidel:* pretty girl. The words are feathers on air—*mameloshn*, the mother tongue, migrates to me.

Wings

That late summer night, I stole my brother's wax and feather wings and strapped them under my breasts and to my arms— oh, the weight was humbling, but I was going to fly before he did. Icarus had taunted me all my life. Called me stupid, a stupid little girl. I readied myself in the rustling fields, the ones behind the olive trees, the harvest only a few weeks off, the smell of grasses all around and the moon full, ripe, commanding the western sky. I had dreamed many dreams that I could fly. My father may have made these wings for my brother, but as the winds picked up, I tilted my head back and spread their magnificence wide—I was in the air all at once, and soon enough, over the trees—and they were my wings. I flew neither too high nor too low, but far across the fields and woods and sea, and all of me, legs, arms, heart, beat with wings that shimmered and shone.

•

The next day, at noontime, when Icarus flew and the crowds cheered, egging his showmanship on, I couldn't help but feel a certain satisfaction or thrill as he aimed higher, nearer the sun, ignoring the warnings of our father because he knew better; he always knew better.

•

Oh, Icarus plunged into the sea, and you would think me a heartless younger sister, yet I knew the secret to the wings: fly alone, fly by the moon, fly as if you are in a dream.

A Brooklyn Walk

For Melissa Broder

*P*acific Street, my daughter reads. "Are we going to the ocean?" she asks. *Indoor garage for rent.* "Do they park cars in their living room?" *Primera Iglesia Bautista.* "See, I can speak Spanish too." A school and a playground with diggers and dirt and dust and "Do the kids get to help move the earth?" *Atlantic Avenue.* "Are we going to the ocean now?" *Works perfectly.* "Why did someone leave their TV under this tree with this sign? Would you abandon me? What kind of tree is this?" *Speed bump.* "Does it thump? Make you jump, jump, jump? And why is that man lighting a cigarette near me? I'm holding my breath. I'm not breathing. Can you tell that I'm not breathing? I'm rounding the corner. Can you see me? Are you coming? When did you get so slow? You're not dying, are you?" *Hoyt Street.* "What's a Hoyt? Hey, a lady is smoking here too. Don't worry, no one's stealing my breath. Are you coming? Can you see me, Momma? Hurry. Are you breathing?"

Derecho

The red fox bolts across Spring Road and stops in the middle of the street. She doesn't realize that I will brake for her, that I've done that for less than her. Once I stopped short for a white plastic bag, thinking it was a toddler, remembering the afternoon waiting for my son's kindergarten bus with my two-year-old daughter—she leapt from my grasp, and somehow I froze; I couldn't even call out for her. I could only watch her aim her compact self, a bright dot, toward the yellow bus, and then she wasn't there, not in the street, not in my sight. From out of nowhere, a silver-haired woman raced forward and grabbed her before she was struck down by the school bus. After that afternoon, I never saw that woman again, yet she made me believe in God or angels for a while. So when the fox, its fiery tail bristling, braces itself in front of my car and shifts its long nose toward me, as if daring me to strike, I want to reassure her. I don't intend to hit her, but why don't I slow down?

I no longer wait for my son or daughter's school bus; the kids, now teenagers, are not allowed out, not without me. We live in an area called, appropriately, Fox Hills West, one of the nicer neighborhoods, if I can give myself that, and it's not unusual to see red-tailed foxes, or deer, or hawks dipping out of the clouds, as if challenging the fighter jets with their tails of white smoke. Ten or twenty feet ahead, the fox presses down into the pavement, as if invisibility is possible.

A year ago, my husband urged me to apply for passports, for the kids, for myself, and I put it off, believing the rhetoric: the policies were aimed at others. "We can't be the last," he said. He had an official blue passport. He was the one who always made sure we had a ready emergency bag. I used to be more afraid of the moments before a storm—the greenish-black skies, the wildly genuflecting trees, the swallows of ozone—than the actual storm. That last night I wished for another storm as he eased my hips next to his, to make love to him, our mouths tasting of the last of the tequila—the last, another unintended consequence of the border closing sixteen years ago. If the night was calm, our lovemaking was calmer, muted, belying the tequila burning our throats.

Before he left, my husband double-checked our supplies, reassuring me that he was only going on ahead to prepare the way. Bottled waters, flashlights with working batteries, Tupperware containers of almonds and beef jerky, extra blankets, and he was gone in the middle of the night, skirting the citizen patrols in our neighborhood twenty miles north of DC, while I pretended to sleep. Since then, forty days and nights, no word from him.

The fox. Maybe she isn't simply a fox. I've heard of tracking drones embedded in dogs and cats. Only a few seconds have passed since I first spotted the fox, or she, me. I am sure it's female, a vixen, watchful, cautious, thinking of its pups in the woods behind our houses. I shouldn't be driving so fast, even though the neighborhood is desolate at this time of day. I shouldn't attract attention. We are among the last folks here who are not party members, and passports are now only for party members.

Ahead of me, in the middle of this placid suburban street, on this fine spring day after the previous night's storm, the red fox isn't the only one deliberating on her chances of escape. Branches are strewn everywhere; the air is dense with seeds and pollen. All this is the result of last night's *derecho*, fierce winds and rain, driven off the mountains as if by angry gods. I bore witness by pressing my body in all its fiery middle-aged nakedness to the upstairs bedroom window and willing the winds to come for me too. I cried out, "I have stayed too long," and I tore up the pane and gave myself up to the frenzy of the derecho.

Slow down. Preserve gasoline. I ease off the pedal and the family's SUV rolls forward like a tired beast. Gossip is fishing boats could still be procured on the Eastern Shore; but I've also heard the bridge is closed to unofficial traffic. I don't know what to believe. I've lost my faith. I am meeting a second cousin of my husband, who claims he knows a guy who can get the kids and me out in exchange for— *what*? Whatever he wants—money will be the first ask. I will be brave.

Ahead of me, the fox quivers, debating its chances of survival. I brake. I pound the wheel and the animal doesn't move. I lay my palm down on the horn and make the car howl.

Inside the Bureaucracy of My Mind

Declutter. Obsess over notes and stacks and anything that can be pruned away. Anything that can't be archived is discarded. Desolate spaces and dust delineate the before and after. Google *depression*, and discover a list of activities that include *watch a funny movie*. The world declares I am 'outstanding' in my productivity; therefore, I can't stop and decode whether a film is highbrow or low decadence. Kale and blueberries and brisk walks are also recommended. Delist. Advertisements for drugs deluge every social media stream. Denude search engine. Read the black-boxed warnings. Dear Depression, dear D., this delicate pill is followed by nausea, diarrhea, inertia, distress, and early death. The body decries the mind. Decamp into the brittle morning sunshine and desiccate weeds in the driveway; they are stubborn, determined to live, dense with the smell of dank earth. With an inherited putty knife I dig into the cracks, scatter slugs and ants and ticks, stab roots from concrete, or the seeds will ascend again, will probably do so anyway. Deliver me. Concentrate; clear it all out. Hear Dad's voice in my head: *Hard work never killed anybody, Toots.* Feel better. Until next time.

The D.C. Mechanic

Why do I fall in love with mechanics? Men who can assure me that it's only the alternator, or the starter, or both. "When was the last time you replaced the battery?" he asks, this one younger than my hometown auto mechanic, and olive-skinned and tattooed. He squints at my car, broken down in front of my rented house, appraising it—the back seat is littered with library books to return and plastic water bottles to recycle and Lego pieces like glitter. It all seems to get away from me these days. "My car has 120,000 miles on it," I'm quick to say. "Don't worry," he says, "it's going to hit 200,000, a car like this." He has a deep singsong way of talking, like a beery country song. As he bends to the underbelly, he lets out a long low whistle at what only he can see. If I break down, I think, this man will know what to do, and I don't mean my car. He won't stand by— he won't say, "What is it *now*?" as if I cry all the time, which I don't. "250,000 miles," he says, standing up and adjusting himself. "I've known cars like this that are still on the road at 300,000. Just take care of it; you hear what I'm saying? Change the oil every few months and the brake pads, and it'll last." After a moment of quiet between us, where he climbs into the cab of his truck and I step back from the curb, he adds, "You'll call me one day, if I'm lying about that mileage, won't you?" He maneuvers his tow's tire lift to the front bumper and secures the axle and wheel suspension before driving off, my car hitched to his truck on its way to repair.

The Critique Group

We talk about giving birth and menopause, about celebrities we would jump in bed with if we had the opportunity, about being married forever from one of us, and not having a date in eighteen months, shit, maybe more—and about your grandmother: How is she? Her home in Chevy Chase is being sold. Ninety years old, and my parents have decided that she cannot live alone anymore—the unreliable furnace and those long flights of stairs leading to all those unopened rooms. We gather closer to her, the youngest among us, and urge her to write more, about her grandmother, about what matters and what terrifies. What we think to ourselves: *How did we find one another?* How lucky we are—four women poised between twenty-nine and fifty. What we say aloud: "We should meet more often." We drink more wine, weep, scream, beat our fists against one another, laugh while gulping for air, a certain power in us to write about anything. And he always arrives late, slick with sweat, riding his bicycle on even the coldest of nights, changing the pheromones in the wide-open room. When he says, "Did I miss anything?" We say, "We haven't even started."

CODA

Little Bear's Apgar Score

The baby is beautiful, but then isn't every baby?

But it's not really beautiful. Its face is red, and its head is oversized, swollen, and dripping with newborn hair and blood.

"Is it?" says one nurse to another.

"Is it what?" Jane screams.

"Look at its toes," instructs the doctor.

"Let me see her feet," Jane implores. Her husband looks even more confused and startled than usual. "What's wrong? Find out what's wrong!" Jane is flat on her back, restrained with IVs. Minutes before, she was the important one—giving birth, undergoing IVF (four cycles in two years), shooting herself up like an addict on a jag with fertility drugs—and now she's abandoned.

She smells blood—*her* blood, the placenta. She struggles to sit up but can't even lift her head. She wants to see how she looks—it can't be good.

"All the tests," she shouts at the ceiling. "I took them all." Jane is forty-four years old; this baby will be her first and only, and she researched it all: the possibility of genetic defects, of chromosomal abnormalities, all of it. She knew the risks were high at her age, but she was having this baby.

"Get her!" Jane orders her husband. She had already warned him that she expected him to be the kind of father that was there for his child. They had only been married a little over two years. Both of them had given up on ever finding someone, and then at a conference, they had noticed one another. Almost out of exhaustion, they decided it was good enough: the conversation at the hotel bar, how they looked together, the sex.

But in recent weeks she suspected him of having an affair with a coworker even though he said that they "are only friends and have been for years." Nine months pregnant, she had followed him to his Friday happy hour and spied on him among a gaggle of other computer geeks. It all looked innocent.

From a corner booth, hidden from their sight, she stroked her stomach, sipped seltzer, and thought she heard the baby speaking to her: "I'm hungry, do you hear me? Let's go home and eat the pizza in the fridge—not the pepperoni slices, the mushroom ones. You can warm it up if you want, or I'll just eat it as is."

The voice finally pushed her up and out the door, insisting, "I'm hungry. Now. Eat something, do you hear me?" On the street, Jane approached a food truck crowded with men, the smell of meat appealing and nauseating. She pushed her stomach to the front of the line and gobbled up a gyro to quiet her.

"They're examining her," her husband says, sweating, the blue scrubs stuck to his tee shirt and shorts. "They're doing the Apgar test."

Her first test. She had to pass it—even though Jane had promised herself that she wasn't going to be that mother who obsessed over grades and SAT scores.

"What is going on? What's taking so long? This is our child; you have to be more assertive. Start now."

"Please, Janey, sweetie, calm down. They're working on her." Working on her—like she was car in need of a new plug or tire.

They didn't have a name for her yet. They had been arguing

over names—Lucy for her mother, Abigail after his mother. They had tried other names and realized that celebrities had taken them all—Shiloh and Vivienne (Angelina Jolie), Seraphina (Jennifer Garner)—and she had despaired: there were no other names left.

The baby's mewing cries turn high-pitched. Jane's heart leaps—and without warning, her breasts leak clear fluid, so close to blood.

"She's such a striking baby," says the doctor. "The look of her startled us."

The nurse hands the swaddled baby to him; the baby wails.

"Give her to me," Jane insists. He slides the baby into her arms. Her little girl is howling, struggling against the blue-and-white blanket's restraints. She had received a ten on the Apgar, a perfect score. Her eyes open and glare at Jane, as if indignant at the prodding and questioning, and then the baby speaks again: "Where exactly am I? And by the way, the name is Ursula. Is there food here? Don't you think I'd be hungry after all that?"

Jane smiles at her, placing Ursula at her breast. This is her beautiful baby.

Shelley and Harvey
Long Island, New York

Shelley was the one who married Harvey right out of college, whose parents went into debt for the wedding, saying it was worth it—that *he* was worth it, they should have said. She had two children, and they bought a house on the south shore of Long Island near their parents.

The secretary—so classic—became the second wife. He was starting to attend galas and fundraisers, and this second wife was soon out of place—all fake tits, big hair, and double negatives in every other sentence, pointed out Shelley. She had left teaching when she had their son, but after the divorce, returned to the same principal and same school, the roughest public high school in Queens. She loved the students, who hailed from more than a dozen countries.

So, the second wife didn't work out, though she turned out smarter than Shelley. She took him for more money than Shelley ever imagined he had. It was the third wife who was the real trophy wife. Joyce Kim. Tall. Reed thin. Twenty years younger. She had an MBA from a big-name school—not the state school where Shelley had met Harvey and made turbulent, awkward sex on dorm beds. Joyce urged Harvey to move to the sprawling condominium with views of the Hudson snaking off into the distance. Joyce looked appropriate at the galas next to the other firmly middle-aged hedge fund managers and their inconsolably slim, possessive wives.

Joyce never called Shelley like the other one did, wanting to gossip, to mine her insights. What was his favorite dessert? What drove him crazy in bed? Do it on a twin with a thin mattress and scratchy sheets, Shelley would've said. Do it to the Ramones. Don't bother with books—he only reads the business section, like his father used to read only the *Daily Racing Form*. And buy only aisle seats if you go to a show. He's claustrophobic.

"We will all miss Harvey," Joyce said coolly in the call she finally did place to Shelley, a polite call, perfectly acceptable given the terrible circumstances of Harvey's death and the status of the will.

The police immediately went to the second wife, who had apparently been on her boat—the *SUH*, or *Screw U Harvey*—with a deck of drunken friends off Freeport. "Ain't nobody touching this girl," second wife said with a toss of her head.

The interview between Shelley and the police was perfunctory. No one thought it could be her—the very middle-aged high school English teacher. Not the one with wide hips and haphazardly colored reddish-brown frizz. She had that loud voice and louder laugh. Somehow the divorce hadn't diminished her. Her kids adored her. She had loads of friends. No one thought that Harvey had ever found his way back to her, craved her more as time went on, wanted only to bury his face in her breasts—does it have to be said that they were always generous, and now, with two kids, with time and gravity, even more so?

There was nothing to do except make love at that motel on Hempstead Turnpike by the hospital every Friday in the late afternoon. That last time, they blasted their music out of an ancient boom box, the grinding of trucks and buses and bursts of Spanish from the bus stop a second track. Ambulances sped by.

They did it once, then poured more of their favorite cheap wine into plastic cups and did it again, the rock-hard pint of Chubby Hubby, his favorite dessert, by the bedside melting, and Harvey panting, sweating, his arms and knees giving out. The smells in the room blended together: disinfectant, roach spray, the sweat of skin on skin. Shelley wanted to make love on top. And after a minute or two, he tried to shove her off—with blood surging to his face and a frantic rebalancing of arms and legs. "You're too much," he said, groaning, laughing, crying, a poetic confluence of emotions. "You were always too fuckin' much for me. That was always the problem."

Shelley thought that he was alive when she left him sprawled on the narrow bed, a shackling of white sheets tangled around his neck and across his face; she really did, didn't she?

No Mercy

No electronic devices, no papers, no pens, no caps, no water bottles, no coffee cups, no gum. No windows. No talking. "No talking!" repeats the bailiff to you and your mother. No sounds, except the buzzing of the fluorescent lights like a swarm of bees over a flat sea, are heard. No odors, except the smell of antiseptic and metallic, frigid air barring the summer morning heat, are evident. No judge, not yet. No girls. A hearing room full of mothers or grandmas with sons or grandsons dressed in jeans or khakis. No shorts, no tank tops, no flip-flops permitted. It's as if the word had gone out: *Bring your son to court today*. Nothing to think about except why you are here as the bailiff says, "All rise," and the judge hurries in from a side door. She's a black lady, in a judge's robe, with high hair and sea green reading glasses hung around her neck, followed by a prosecutor, her head barely floating above her stack of files. Your mother whispers, "Stand up straight."

The judge eases behind a wide desk, not a bench, not like a TV judge. The bailiff continues, "You will be called up alphabetically, and you and your counsel, if you have counsel, should approach the bar." A low gate separates the judge from the rest of you like you were dogs. Last instructions from the bailiff: "Plaintiff and counsel only to the bar."

This means: You don't get to bring your mother to the judge.

You are eighteen. The age of majority. This isn't juvenile court.

"Eyes forward," says a cop, stopping near you and your mother in the last row. He's part of the frenzy of police in the hearing room.

Your head hangs low. Long Beach is less than ten minutes from here with its boardwalk and your friends. Your girlfriend, Angelique, who likes getting high even more than you, would usually be there by now, the early morning sun warming her.

"Hands where I can see them," the cop continues, bearing down on you. Your fingers, with their nails bitten to the whites, suck like starfish to rocks over your banged-up kneecaps. If she could, Angelique would surely be here for you.

Your mother attempts an appealing smile towards the cop. Her round sad face glistens. She used to be pretty before she let herself get gray-haired and fat. She scoops her hands onto her lap, as if she's done something wrong. The cop circles off to the back of the courtroom.

Up front, the bailiff announces the first name and your mother listens intently, as if you will miss your turn. Your last name is no longer hers. She has scattered the remains of your father and a second husband off the far end of the boardwalk. She says she's afraid that she'll outlive you too.

"Aleman," calls the bailiff and reads out his charges. Aleman's mother adjusts his tie and motions for him to tuck in his shirt. He's stick-thin, his skin the color and texture of driftwood. He trudges behind his lawyer and slumps before the judge.

You didn't realize that the bailiff shouts out the offense, that everyone will know what you are accused of today.

Aleman lets his lawyer plead his case, drug possession, and the lawyer is slick and simpering. The judge doesn't smile back. His lawyer protests that the fine is unfair. The judge says that he should just continue and she'll double it, "if that's what you want. You let me know, and I'll go higher." The bam-bam-bam of her gavel reverberates to the back of the room. Aleman laughs, the idiot. But for some reason, you think it's funny too.

Your mother flinches. She must be thinking about how much today will cost. She had to take another day off from her summer teaching job. The rent hasn't been paid in two months. These days, she doesn't even open the bills on the kitchen table.

"Alvarez," calls the bailiff. Alvarez has a mother plus a girlfriend or wife with a baby in her arms. The infant, wrapped snug in a sky blue blanket, with broad cheeks and shiny eyes, blinks at the lights. After a second of wonder, his eyelids sink, and the girlfriend or wife holds him even closer. DUI. Driving under the influence. Alvarez pleads to the judge that he needs his license for his delivery job. He's sorry, very sorry. The prosecutor shuffles papers and says, "This one's, let me see, got it right here, a first-time offense?" She says this to the judge like it's a question, instead of a statement of fact. Alvarez has no lawyer. He looks like he's been beached, some kind of fish, his mouth opening and closing, searching for water, not air, and you feel sorry for him. "No one hurt?" asks the judge, who receives an affirmative. The baby wails and is escorted out with the girlfriend or wife before Alvarez is given a fine and a warning.

Your mother grips your arm, the one that was broken in three places. She must not know how much she is hurting you. You've already cried over what you did; you don't know if you can ever cry like that again, but maybe if she keeps squeezing.

Instead, she lets go, knits her hands back together. "You go up to that judge, Daniel," she says, "and you ask for compassion and leniency and pity and forbearance and—"

"No talking," the bailiff directs at her, and your mother, the English teacher, must rest her plea.

You don't have a lawyer either. Your shoulders shake. You could use a drink, or more. A hit. The main door to the hearing room opens, and you tense. *Angelique.* "I'm so sorry," says the slip of a girl as all eyes turn toward her. She is dark-haired, bare-armed, unmoored. A cop hurries to secure the door.

You love the beach, the roar of the ocean and rip of high tide, the taste of salt on skin, the sense of being inside the sea and its shell, even when you are not high. When you were three or four years old, your father would balance you on his shoulders and wade into the waves, one of the few memories you have of the man. You want to run after the girl, who looks enough like Angelique, and confess this all to her. You're ready to bolt when your mother begs, "Mercy. You ask for mercy." You stay. Eyes forward. Hands where you can see them.

You've promised your mother that you'd do better. You couldn't even finish your first year of college. You met Angelique on the boardwalk, and she was the answer, along with her fast car and getting high. Eventually, when you drove onto the sand after midnight, you knew that doing so was illegal. And veering into the waves, which leapt toward the full moon—she swore to you that her car could ride on water—you were sure that the ocean would carry you on its shoulders.

You should have drowned then. As the horseshoe crabs and silver fish and cold-searing sea rushed in, you were so high you shouted that it must be a joke, Poseidon's revenge. And Angelique didn't follow; after you smashed the side window and swam out, she stayed, anchored to her seat. After all these weeks, she is still unresponsive, in the intensive care unit at the County Hospital.

Forget the hearing and the judge and the bond. Better that you go to jail. To prison. Get clean there, far from the boardwalk, far from the sea.

You sweat cold. Chew off your nails, swallow the scabrous skin, and feel the rising tide of blood pounding in your heart: No mercy.

Counting Backwards

10. If you can count backwards from 10, you are not drunk.

9. It now takes two bottles of wine to get drunk. I only drink wine. Today the *Wall Street Journal* confirms that women drink more wine than men do. Unlike Joanne, who changed her name for the *Wall Street Journal* story, I don't hide my wine bottles. The garbage men who sling our cans from curb to truck before six in the morning are fine, lusty men.

8. I never drink Monday to Thursday. Those are school nights. Sometimes I cheat and drink on Thursday nights because, fuck it, I'm not in school anymore.

7. I am horrified to read about mothers caught driving drunk with their children. This week, a forty-two-year-old grandmother in our nearby suburban town was caught drunk with her grandchildren in the car. I'm not sure if I'm more horrified that she was drunk or that she was forty-two and a grandmother. I had twins at forty-two. I hate my smugness.

6. I know I should eat a little something when I drink. If I were French or Italian, I'd naturally have a glass of wine with dinner. Pregnant women in Europe even drink wine. I don't drink with dinner. Sometimes I don't even eat dinner. I didn't drink at all when I was pregnant, not one drop.

5. I watch my husband eat steak: very well done, not an ounce of blood. He cuts into the meat with the sharpest knife in the house and grins at me. He likes when I cook for him. My son and daughter eat sticky macaroni and cheese with their fingers. I want to lick their fingers clean, but they will think Mommy is weird.

6. My husband joins me in a glass of chilled white wine, a summery Moscato. We open all the windows in the living room and turn off the lights. The scents of cherry blossoms and cut grass sieve through the screens. We ask one another again if we miss our other life, in the city, before the kids, and neither of us answers because we do.

7. We say to one another for the hundredth time that we have done the right thing: moved to the suburbs, had me freelance, had the kids (asleep now). They are the most right. The most right, my brain repeats in the dark. I refill my glass. My husband groans, "What a week." I say, "I expect sex." He pushes his glass away with a dramatic, I'll-get-ready flair. "Do you want to make love or drink?" "If I had sex every night like we used to I wouldn't need to drink," I say, and recognize the rationalization like a punch in the gut. I finish off his glass as well as my own.

8. I once drove my car to Shopwell after drinking two or three glasses of wine—no children in the car. Buzzed, I suddenly had the urge for French vanilla ice cream. At the traffic light, I blared a classic rock radio station. I stroked the cold box of Breyers. I saw a shadow with a turban cross the road from his Sikh temple to the Dunkin' Donuts. Ahead of me, at least fifty yards, a car careened down the

street, a fat car. I swear I heard the crash, the peel of tires, but saw nothing else in the blur of the evening. The next day I read that a Sikh was killed crossing Main Street and anyone with any knowledge should call this special hotline number. My head hurt.

9. We have sex and afterwards I pour myself another glass of wine. He's sleeping. I'm still horny. I count backwards from ten. I'm not drunk enough.

10. I had no idea who Sikhs were. On a morning without any other projects, I researched: "The essence of Sikh teaching is summed up in these words: Realization of Truth is higher than all else. Higher still is truthful living." A neighbor reported that his neighbor's car, which had always been meticulously cared for, had a broken headlight, a dent, and scarring. A sixty-five-year-old long-time resident was arrested for involuntary manslaughter and driving while intoxicated. I felt sick. I never ate French vanilla ice cream again. I licked my children's fingers. They tasted like dirt and butter. I even stopped drinking wine, for a while.

Beheaded

An American is beheaded. We have so many ways to kill one another, but even the word 'beheaded' beckons to another time. I cannot recall the last time I read it in a modern context. Why not use 'decapitate,' or would that sound too much like something Freddie or Chucky would do? In Syria or Iraq, another person is beheaded, head bagged, and another, on bent knees. Beheaded. A black-masked killer. This Old English word backs into the evening news beat. I would like to advocate breathing new life into 'betrothed,' or 'beloved.'

Buttons

I can't speak for John, usually called Button. I can't tell you exactly what happened to him after he was bequeathed by Major Lawrence Lewis to his daughter Frances Park Butler, of the Butler family of Louisiana, the Officers of the American Revolution Butlers, the cotton and sugar plantation Butlers.

To return to John, usually called Button: Major Lewis in his *Last Will and Testament*, a finely written letter, the original on file in the courthouse in Fairfax, Virginia, bequeaths Nelly, Dennis, Tom, George, Jane, Mary, Frances (not the daughter, the names for the enslaved were some of the same as the owners) and Lucinda, along with "John, usually called Button," to his daughter, Frances Park Butler. A copy of his *Last Will and Testament* was discovered by me, a writer-in-residence, in the clamorous green steel file cabinets upstairs, in the backrooms of the Woodlawn estate, the house where John was being willed from, the place where people knew him as 'Button.'

A broad-chested boy with big soft brown eyes, that's how I pictured him. But he could have been six-foot-tall, strong enough to unload the barges that travelled on the canal locks along the Potomac. Or perhaps he was fast enough to race to meet the weekly postal service, which was delivered along US 1 outside the plantation, and return before Miss Nelly finished her sweet tea, which was always served with a sprig of mint pinched fresh, if possible, from the kitchen garden.

Sometimes John, usually called Button, would chew on wild

mint leaves to stupor his hunger. In the will, however, there is no indication of ages. A young man would make more sense, wouldn't it? Button is a child's name, isn't it? John, usually known as Button, with his wide coffee-cream eyes.

In the third paragraph of Major Lawrence's will it states exactly this: "Thirdly, I confirm to my said daughter the right and title to the following slaves given to her by her mother Nelly—that is to say: Nelly, Dennis, Tom, George, Jane, Mary, Frances, John, usually called Button, and Lucinda and their increase." *Their increase*. The generations after them.

John, usually called Button, arrived at Donboyne Plantation on the banks of the Mississippi near the village of Bayou Goula on November 25, 1835. Frances wrote about the arrival of her inheritance in a letter, a copy of which rests in the steel file too.

I pray that John, usually called Button, ran soon after he arrived in Louisiana. Hid in a steamer going up the Mississippi. Ran west to Texas and down to Mexico. Ran into the wintery snows of the Midwest, to St. Louis and beyond. I pray he dropped the 'Button' and renamed himself so the slave catchers and their dogs could not find him, or just claimed 'John' as his name, because that was a name he heard in Bible readings, because that is a man's name. In fact, I'm going to be sure nobody tracked John down. He's among us now; we can feel his eyes on us.

•

When Elizabeth was cleaning, and she always seemed to be working on Woodlawn when she was here —the eighteenth-century estate bred bric-a-brac in its musty corners—she discovered the button in the back of the closet in the upstairs bedroom, the one with the winter view of the Potomac, the bedroom where the Marquis de Lafayette once slept.

Elizabeth sighed, fanning the beads of perspiration from her neck and collarbone, and across the scoop of her blush-pink work dress. Elizabeth Montgomery Sharpe liked costumes, galas, and even, on occasion, the libertine extravaganza with a piano player banging out rhythms, ragtime music (though her good friend Alice Roosevelt had them play "Maple Leaf Ragtime" at the White House this year, so perhaps in 1906 ragtime is not that scandalous anymore), and she liked ragtime juke tune dancing, smoking the marijuana, some opium, and men dancing with women, men with men, and women, oh, with women.

But this morning, in the vast quiet of Woodlawn, Elizabeth wore her I-will-organize-the-closets dress covered by a crisp white apron. She considered her find: A commemorative button, fairly weightless in her palm even if it was brass. Stamped with an eagle, underneath it read: "Memorable Era March the Fourth 1789." This was the incorrect date of George Washington's first inaugural; however, Elizabeth didn't know that at this moment.

Elizabeth wasn't surprised at finding the button in the corner of the closet. Since the turn of the century Elizabeth owned Woodlawn, a piece of American history, falling down as it was. Woodlawn had originally been the home of Nelly Parke Custis, the favorite granddaughter of Martha Washington, adopted granddaughter of George. Nelly had married George's nephew, Lawrence Lewis, son of George's sister, Betty, and the General had given them this land carved from Mt. Vernon, his own plantation. Unfortunately, Lawrence Lewis couldn't make a go of farming, and the estate was sold to Northerners, and worse—to the townspeople up in Alexandria, home to one of the largest slave markets—to Quakers, who in their high-minded way experimented with free labor (Elizabeth knew all about dealing with hard-backed men—her father made his fortune with anthracite mines in Pennsylvania). Eventually, the Quakers gave up on the plantation too, and the house and all its acreage eventually ended up purchased by her dear, dreamy playwright and novelist, Paul Kester.

Dust. Dust. Dust.

None of the men improved anything. She had to do all the real work. Electricity. Bathrooms. She had to preserve history and make the present presentable and livable and without a right to vote, or even the right to own this property without her father's co-signature on the damn deed. She swatted at cobwebs.

Elizabeth Montgomery Sharpe wanted a place in history too. Was that why she used her fortune to buy this estate from Kester? What could this commemorative button be worth? She plunked it into her apron pocket. When she could, she'd bring it over to Mount Vernon and let one of those cantankerous curators take a look at it; or maybe she'd just wear it on a red, white, and blue ribbon and parade up and down the banks of the Potomac, naked and free with George Washington's eagle flying between her breasts.

•

I have my own story about buttons. My dad's father, my grandfather—near the end of his life, after owning a chicken farm in New Jersey; after immigrating from Paris; and before that, Palestine when it was a British Mandate; and before that, his place of birth: Chercoz in the Ukraine—owned a notions store on Nostrand Avenue in

Brooklyn, New York. The store sold yards of cloth, spools of thread, sewing needles, and buttons. In the front, buttons were displayed in packets of six and twelve, and I was not permitted to touch those buttons.

However, past the bolts of cloth, which were laid out like bodies in a catacomb, in the back room was a curio stocked with more buttons, hundreds of buttons, thousands of buttons. The curio had a dozen drawers, and inside a panoply of buttons of every color and size. Some were smooth as river stones, some smelled smoky, a few were dotted with pearls or diamonds—fake, but not to me.

Up front, neighborhood ladies, who hailed from the Caribbean, haggled, buying cloth for the cataclysm of winter months. The women's voices rang high, my grandfather sprinkled French, Spanish, and Yiddish with English, and somehow cloth was cut, sewing needles selected, coins parsed. Sales were made on a register that rattled every time a sale was rung.

"May I have a button, Daddy?" my seven-year-old self asked my father, who had come to borrow money and was put to work on this Saturday afternoon.

"Ask your grandfather," he said.

This grandfather, with his bent back, with the white hairs spiraling out of his ears and nose, with the accent, often forgot that his granddaughter spoke only one language. He growled at me, and my father screamed, "English, Pop. English."

Grandpa looked like he didn't know how this girl with a bone-yellow wood button cupped in her hand could be related to him. His family only had sons. He was one of five, or perhaps six brothers, all of whom stayed behind in Chercoz except for him, all of whom were murdered in the Second World War. By luck, he had two sons in America. No one he knew had girls, so who was this little one? How could she have survived the war that took his mother and all the others? Where did she come from? She has had his mother's high cheekbones, her eyes like a doe from the Duke's forest. He glanced about—his store was on a bustling street in Brooklyn, the forest far from here.

The girl has a smell about her like autumn, like apples. Every Jewish New Year his mother would make apple cakes. As the youngest, he'd climb the highest branches and toss down the fruit to his brothers before the Duke's men and their dogs caught the scent of the boys and the stolen ripe red apples. His hand trembled over the cash register. *What can I offer her to go?*

"Grandpa? Can I have this button?" I asked.

"Take," he said, finding his English, and dismissing me, "Take all the buttons."

Slant Rhyme

The poet leading the workshop approaches the poetry of old wars, of Walt Whitman in the Civil War and Wilfred Owen in World War I, with pure concentration, dissecting and disassembling lines, and it is like Deborah is listening through ether. She can't respond to his questions, or properly formulate her own. Once in her life, she met a Navy cadet on campus during a football game, Navy versus Syracuse. The cadet said she could try on his white hat if she kissed him.

She kissed him.

•

Enjambment and rules of engagement—he is talking poetry, not war, even though he is mixing terms. He has published two chapbooks of poetry while a Navy surgeon. He is currently in the reserves, which means in the last two years he's performed surgery in Afghanistan and Iraq. He also references his age, ten years older than she is, but she isn't young either, though sometimes she forgets that. Sometimes she believes she still could fall for a guy who loved words, a guy who carried battered notebooks crammed with ideas, even though those same men became insurance brokers or Navy surgeons.

•

Enjambment—a line in poetry without punctuation. He snatches at the air with long fingers and scrubbed square nails. He has memorized the poems. She makes the mistake of telling him that she has read his chapbooks. He directs the words more at her than at the others. William Carlos Williams was a doctor too, she points out. He dismisses her comment as flattery, which it is.

•

End-stopping— the opposite of enjambment. He lulls her with his singsong recitations, full of twangs like he is a bluegrass singer, like he should have a banjo or a slide guitar. He jabs to the air above her head in meter, to the stressed syllable. She sucks in her breath, pulls in the muscles of her stomach, and forces herself to stop thinking of him cupping her breasts as he continues leading the discussion of prosody. With all the silence around her these days, the sound of his voice rushes through her. Her nipples go hard, as if the room is cold.

•

Rhyme. "Did he believe in rhyme? Does someone need to believe in what children believe?" He is musing and she is falling for it. He's dressed in a deep blue button-down shirt and crisp blue jeans and brilliant white sneakers. He has hair like a helmet, like the current vice president of the United States. She can forgive him the hair if he can forgive that she is dressed in all black—a pilled sweater, well-worn leggings—which always worked in Manhattan, but not down here. She has learned that much in the past two months, since she moved to the suburbs outside Washington D.C., that women down here like their colors, blues and reds and yellows like flags on ships at sea. They like to talk about the accomplishments of their children and are vague about what their husbands do—consultants, most of them. She doesn't know how to ask the follow-up question—"Consulting on what?"—without appearing too much the outsider, something she's felt all her life.

The Navy surgeon/poet has good strong teeth. She can picture him in his Navy whites. Gold buttons. Medals, even.

"Ma'am, your poems read like somebody who has a lot of secrets. Do you have a lot of secrets?"

"None," Deborah replies quickly. "Absolutely none."

•

After the workshop, on the way across the campus to the panel with more famous poets, she asks, "Children? I only ask because you mentioned nursery rhymes in class."

"Grown," he says. "Thank goodness. I am no admirer of the facetious rhyme so often found in children's books."

"A wife?"

He roars in laughter at her directness. She's a New Yorker, she says, as if that's the reason for the blunt questions.

"No, ma'am. Divorced. All my fault too."

She can't tell if he's using 'ma'am' with irony or not, whether he's teasing her with a degree of subservience, or superiority. She yearns to go back to prosody. She hopes that he doesn't ask about her husband—the insurance broker, dead—or her child—gone, Seattle.

And then he adds, eagerly, "I've taken a vow of chastity as a direct result, but I'm going to end that soon."

She's been formulating a question about slant rhymes for him since the workshop ended. She should ask it now, but it doesn't feel like the right follow-up to chastity.

Slant rhymes: also known as imperfect rhyme, half-rhyme, near-rhyme, lazy rhyme, or oblique rhyme, formed by words with similar but not identical sounds. Eyes/ light. Years/ yours. These rhymes are not quite what they seem to be; is that the secret to slant rhymes?

•

He's a sixty-year-old Navy surgeon/poet who has taken a vow of chastity. Wasn't that for young girls in places like Utah? She didn't want to demean any girls from Utah. She liked Utah, in particular Park City, with its annual independent film festival, which she attended in her other life, the one she left back in Manhattan before coming here to work at the Library of Congress on the National Film Registry and film preservation. These days, her life is filled with silent movies.

This man beside her, however, was married for twenty years and has two grown daughters, and he hasn't had sex in two years. "I am saving myself for a revelation," he continues.

She never saved herself for anything.

•

"Why did you take my workshop?"

"Who wouldn't want to take a class on war poetry." She tries not to sound weary saying this. She hadn't been talking much lately, and all the effort, all morning, was bearing down on her.

"Pardon me, ma'am, but you were the only one who sent in poems."

"I follow instructions." She decides that she doesn't like being called 'ma'am'; it reminds her that she is not from here. "Call me Deborah."

"Debbie, I read your poems."

"Deborah."

"There are things I can teach you."

"I'm open to anything."

•

He breaks the silence, sharing with her that he took his vow of chastity along with one of devotion in Jerusalem. "Have you ever been? To Jerusalem."

"No, not yet." Maybe someday when she can pray at the Western Wall with the men, but she doesn't say that. She doesn't feel ready to confess to him that she is a Jew, one of those eternally questioning Jews, a nonbeliever in the patriarchal constructions of theology, a woman whose husband died too young, someone who believes that the power of God lies in the imperfect, not the perfect, and even so, she really just signed up for this literary conference because she was lonely and lost in her new city.

"Everyone should go," he says.

She'll go. After this power-walk, she'll be in shape to climb Masada.

"I had a revelation there." She's not going to ask him for details. They are late for the panel discussion. "Did you ever have a revelation?" he asks her.

She couldn't be less comfortable if he asked her if she had an orgasm lately. She'd give the same answer. Nevertheless, she'll admit it: she wonders what it would be like to be the first to break his vow, to wrinkle up his pressed shirt and pants and ruffle that white hair. She'd make him recite more Whitman in that southern twang of his, or William Carlos Williams, the poem about plums, sweet and cold. She licks her lips. Let those words fly from his precise, razor-thin lips.

"Ma'am, Jerusalem is the place to have it. I had mine at The Church of Holy Sepulchre. My revelation was to commit myself to doctoring and…" Deborah wonders if he is going to say poet-ing, but he says, "writing."

•

"Did you ever hear of Jerusalem Syndrome?" he asks, lengthening his stride. She matches him. "Apparently, people go there and go a little crazy, have all kinds of what you'd might call revelations. I was there on my knees, tearing at my chest, shouting down the Almighty. I had questions, heart-rendering, splitting-wood, wrecking-havoc questions."

He stops so she does too, even though she realizes that she needs to get where she is going now. He breathes hard and fast, working himself up. And all of her is suddenly damp with the sweep of prickly heat, a fire lit under her skin. She doesn't know when she got old, but at this moment, she feels all her cells and scents surface, the smell of clinging wool on raw skin. He must think it's him—he angles toward her as if he can smell her hormones hollowing out.

•

"Am I going to have the privilege of reading more of you?" he asks as they reach the auditorium. "Will you send me more of your work? It will be its own revelation."

Her black sweater is limp with sweat. Her hair springs to life, wild about her face, and she feels feral, infused with ideas. He's watching her chest rise and fall. She wonders if he is going to check her pulse, ask about her blood pressure. He doesn't sweat. He still doesn't have a white hair out of place, a crease wrinkled, a sneaker marked.

"I'm going to work on slant rhyme," she says with more confidence in her own words than she's had in a long time. "On the imperfect."

Deborah marches past him and grabs open a side door to the auditorium. Gathered on the stage is the panel of famous poets. The sound system isn't working well so they are passing one handheld microphone among the four them, acting awed and terrified at the volume of their words, and she is ready with questions.

Sweetness

One bite, that's what I offer Lucia.

The idiot doctor had said I should go home and get some rest. I don't know when I slept last—weeks ago, before her diagnosis.

She'll have a bite, and then I'll finish it, even though I'm a guy who, before I met her, would tell you: I don't like sweets. The dessert is in my hand, and my hand is near her lips, and she must smell the vapors of sugar; she must know I'm here. Dusting powder falls like snow or cocaine on my work shirt.

I hadn't been with Lucia long, just over a year, long enough to not want to sleep without her. We weren't old when we first met; she was just past thirty. Some people think that's still young but she didn't.

She was a girl with curves, that's what I thought the first time I saw her through the open door of the Raven Grill, and then inside, next to me, asking for directions. She was—I mean, she is Italian; she'd say Sicilian, from a village in the mountains outside Palermo, "a place we will visit someday" she said that first night. She was saying this and feeding me bits of *pignoli*, almonds and pine nuts and butter in a cookie, and I was thinking, *You must been have born smelling sweet.* We were only going together a couple of weeks before we got married at City Hall. I soon learned that she swooned over *sfogliatelle, struffoli, tiramisu.* I fumbled with the consonants and vowels in these desserts, maybe even bumbling them on purpose because it made her laugh. She liked to buy these treats from the old-time bakery next to the hipster coffee shop, the bakery that couldn't be bought out when the neighborhood changed, the bakery that still puts your desserts in a cardboard box and pulls down a red and white string from a hive of strings and ties it all up with a double knot. She must have felt like a queen bee swinging those boxes into our apartment on a Friday night. She'd make pasta—"Don't say spaghetti," she'd say—and I'd say, "Oh, oh, spa-get-tio-s," just so she'd get mad, fake mad, and pour us another class of dark red wine and swing her hips.

Lucia never went as far as singing opera, but in my dreams, she did. I spent my whole life listening to rock and punk, and in my dreams when I slept beside her, I heard arias. She never wanted to go out on Friday nights. I spent the years before Lucia at happy hour drinking two-for-one beers and snatching at greasy sliders and wings, suffering the indignities of compulsively checking my phone, as if I had plans, as if someone or something important was coming my way. Nothing did until her, and suddenly on Fridays I was skipping lunch, working out at the gym, going home taut and hungry. The rest of the workweek we would stay late at our respected jobs. Afterwards, we'd meet for something quick, a salad for her, a burger for me. Now on Fridays, I was home drinking wine, eating pasta with homemade sauce, a *biscotti* or *pizzelle* or *tartufo* to end the meal, "to end the week with sweetness," she'd say. Her lips swathed in powdered sugar, we'd make love, and count crumbs in the dwell of her cleavage, and make more love.

And plans, we had plans for that trip to Sicily next fall. Hustling down drugs, which are legal in California and Oregon, to kill my sweetheart, collapsed with *gliobastoma multiforme*, that reeks, that's foul-tasting, that there's no playing around with pronouncing, that means brain tumor, weren't in my plans.

Her dark hair weaves against the white sheets.

Her dark eyes open, and weep.

"One last bite," I say. "You'll only taste the cream of the cannoli. You'll only taste the sugar. And then I'll take a bite, and—" These words heave out of me in a rush, my hand shudders. What I taste is chalk and dust, the world spins and buzzes.

All of her refuses me. Instead, she eases over, doing her best to hide the pain in her bones. I throw away the tainted dessert, scrub my hands, and crawl into bed beside her. She brings the fingers that would have fed her poison to her lips, as if this is the pact: We will both suffer, but not alone, not yet. And I kiss her mouth, and I find the hollow of her sunken breasts, and I sleep.

Gargoyles and Stars

At the corner where Lydia thought she left her car was a lake of crushed glass. She was sure she had parked the car, directly behind the 'no parking from here to corner sign' and 'no parking: construction' sign, which since there wasn't any construction that she could see, she assumed it was fine. She was three blocks from the campus, and a pair of slender, ephemeral students hurried by her. She remembered this for them:

> "The City College of New York, founded as the Free Academy and opened in 1849, began as an educational and political experiment. It was the first public college in New York, and it soon became known as 'The Poor Man's Harvard.'"

As she stood in the gutter where she was sure she had parked her car—she had even written the address down since she was prone to misplacing her parked car these days—she had this vision of herself in a miniskirt and boots in front of prospective freshmen and their parents, a half-remembered self. "But I can't stand here forever, can I?" she said, digging her phone out of the bottom of her purse. The phone was dead. So, no car, no phone. Now if she had a phone she could call one of those Uber cars, even though she had never done that before. Of course, she'd call her husband first.

She could make her way back to the university, her alma mater; there must be a security guard somewhere who could help her. She had driven in for a special evening lecture, and had quite enjoyed it, even though it ran late, and she stayed even later admiring the Gothic architecture of Shepard Hall. So she wasn't going to have the night ruined. *If only there were still pay phones on street corners*, she thought, and then a police car wound its way up the block. She flagged it down. "I think my car was stolen," she said in an even tone to the stony-eyed officer. She didn't want to jump to conclusions. She wasn't going to panic.

"You need to go down to the precinct," he said. "On 125th Street." His radio beeped and flashed, and he waited a minute until she repeated, "125th Street," then left her tracing the burning whir of sirens and lights into the air. She hesitated, studying the gothic peaks of the university against the sky with its crowds of stars over the campus heights. She recited, not a poem, though she certainly knew some poetry:

> "The campus as it now stands was designed by George B. Post in 1898. Post's Collegiate Gothic design was associated with the medieval images of Oxford and Cambridge. See the many grotesque sculptures decorating the building and notice that they are engaged in activities reflecting academic pursuits. Above, a creature reads a book; another pours a substance into a flask during an experiment."

She looked up as if expecting a gargoyle to fly past her.

Ahead of her, the line of parked cars snaked down the curbs of Convent Avenue. Across the street: a new school of architecture, a white, windowless cube, half underground, wedged outside the campus gates. She couldn't bear to look at it. No gargoyles guarded that building. "Well, I'm going to have to get myself to that precinct." However, in addition to there being no phone booths, there were no taxicabs at this time of night in this part of Harlem.

Nevertheless, she was quite capable of walking from 130th to

125th Street, no matter that it was late and the way ahead of her now deserted, canyons of locked doors and shut-tight windows. Harlem was safer now than in her day when squeegee men would gather around flaming garbage cans, passing a bottle, eyeing girls like her. They're all gone. And she had on her comfortable shoes, didn't she? She didn't wear miniskirts or high-heeled suede boots anymore— she joked with herself before double-checking. Her shoes were black and thick-soled, and she wore dark pants with a stretch waist. The night was chilly but she had forgotten a coat. No use waiting here; she was good to go.

•

Lydia arrived about twenty minutes later at the police precinct and climbed the short flight of stairs. She sniffed. The air smelled of old colognes and lingering mildew. She wished she could be back on the street. Her legs and hips ached. Her purse had twisted under her armpit. Her hand clutched a scrap of paper.

You know this address, she thought. Of course, you're a university student. English lit major. Dating a nice guy. Lyddie and Moe, that's what everyone calls you.

His full name is Maurice and yours is Lydia. Moe has a Fu-Manchu mustache, and your mother doesn't like him, yet she is very proud that you're the first in the family to go to college. That's it, isn't it? Cool. Groovy. Dig it. Right on. She wanted to pump her fist in the air.

When the officer on duty finally showed up at the front desk, gray and hook-faced, he gurgled down sips of coffee from one those quart-size containers, one filled with cream and extra sugars, a dizzy steam rising from its core. "I'm here because of my car," said Lydia, pleased at knowing what to say to him even though she was a little muddled. "My car is missing."

"License and registration."

Lydia felt compelled to explain further that she had been at a lecture at City College. She wouldn't want him to think she was in the neighborhood for anything involving drugs. In the past, men and their wet whispers of *smoke, smoke, smoke*, followed her from the subway to the campus. She had smoked a little pot in her day, didn't she? She sucked in her breath. She was sure she did and that she liked it.

The officer gazed down on her. She would have loved a cup of the sweet coffee, to jolt her memory, but instead she said, "At City College, you should know that Dr. Noah Webster, our first president, a graduate of West Point, said that the school was an experiment. 'Whether an institution of the highest grade can be successfully controlled by the popular will, not by the privileged few.'"

"License and registration, and we'll get you out of here."

Lydia wished there was somewhere to sit, but there were no chairs in sight. She paced, planning on how she'd share this with Moe. He was always protective of her, not that he had to be. She'd make it a funny story; tell him about the gargoyles and stars.

When the officer finally returned, he said, "Your car was towed to the pound. Parking at a construction site."

"But I wasn't, was I?" Lydia turned to leave. She had been here long enough.

"Wait just one minute, you'll need these." He pressed toward her a scroll of tickets printed out from some computer along with her license and registration. "You think you should call and tell somebody to come get you?"

Lydia's back bristled. She wasn't going to worry Moe. "What's the address?"

"Pier 76. West 38th Street and 12th Avenue."

"Open now?"

"Open twenty-four hours."

On 125th Street, she hailed a yellow taxicab.

•

At the City of New York tow pound, she found herself in a waiting room that could be anywhere—no windows, the stink of cigarettes, even with the *No Smoking* sign, every seat filled—but at the same time, nowhere but Manhattan. The clock over the service windows read eleven o'clock. It would be one o'clock in the morning before it was her turn, before she'd discover that she had no more cash on her, not even a credit card. One thing the room did have was a bank of pay phones, and one worked. Luckily quarters always speckled the bottom of her purse. She dialed the phone number inside her address book marked smartly 'In Case of Emergency.'

•

Someone ashen and unshaven in sweatpants approached her spot among the pay phones—he wasn't Moe, who liked bell-bottomed jeans and wide-collared shirts, and for all that hair and that mustache had a neat appearance.

"Ma!" he said. "Come on."

She covered up her surprise with "This is how you catch a cold," pointing to his bare feet in sneakers.

"You're killing me, Ma. It's three o'clock in the morning and I get a call that you're at the pound."

Of course, this was her son. Gabriel. "Where's your father?"

"Give me the tickets." He went up to window number three and paid the fines, two hundred and fifty dollars, and then he was shuffling out ahead of her, out the doors, through the maze of towed cars slick with the dank dew of the Hudson River. "Is Moe okay?" she called after him. "Why isn't he here?"

"Because he's dead," Gabriel said, turning left and right, confused amid the rows of cars lined in the wait of dawn.

She wanted to make a joke, to say, "That's the reason?" but she could see that he was haggard and fretful.

"We have to talk about what's next, Ma."

"We're going home."

"I don't live with you anymore, Ma. I'm a fifty-year-old guy."

"Then I'm glad you don't live with me."

"I'm going to drive you back to your house."

"How will you get home?"

"Don't worry about me."

"I'm your mother, aren't I?"

He slammed his fist onto the roof of a car. She hoped it wasn't hers. Tears cracked from his eyes. "There must be a thousand fucking cars here!"

"I'm sorry I called you. I'll find my own car."

He hitched up his sweatpants and huffed around her, sinking in behind the wheel of a vehicle three down from where they had been standing.

"I'll drive," she said, tapping the window.

"Are you kidding me? Get in."

She wanted to say, "Yes, Moe," but remembered that this man wasn't Moe. She climbed into the passenger seat anyway; it felt good to sit.

"For once you're going to listen to me. You got to stop driving back to that campus up in Harlem. It isn't safe."

"Nothing but good things ever happened to me there," she said quietly.

He clutched the dashboard. "I know. You met Dad there. You were campus guides."

"I was pretty good at it too. Better than Moe. More outgoing. Don't get me wrong, Moe is brilliant, a physics major, but I always say to him 'don't hide your face in a crowd of stars. I'll always love you.'" Her thoughts trailed off before shooting back. "When did he die? When did Moe die?"

"A long time ago. I was a kid. He was murdered, buying heroin."

"On campus?"

"No, in Yonkers, not far from the house." He sighed. "You always told me he went straight to heaven."

"Did you know that ten graduates of the City University of New York went on to win Nobel Prizes? They were the children of the working class and often the first of their families to go to college, like many of the students here today."

"You remember all of that, don't you?"

He jammed the key into the ignition. "We're getting out of here," he said, but didn't start the engine.

The sun edged up over the rows of towed cars, over the pilings of the old pier and out toward the Hudson River and the state of New Jersey. The stars faded; they always do. At the same time, she knew they were always there. The Gothic spires and the gargoyles and the entire campus rose over Harlem, and in her sights, a place of hope and possibility—and with all respect to home or heaven, she was fine waiting here.

What I Didn't Carry with Me

"I didn't bring anything with me."

"How could you bring nothing?"

"I don't even remember the month it was. My brother thinks July."

"Nothing? Not a blankie?" I know my husband is remembering our son, with his trailing baby blue boy blanket monogrammed with his initials.

The neighbor gave me her family's green pea soup. So thick it made the spoon heavy. So salty, I could float in that soup, a green sea of soup. If I remember too well, I can feel green pea soup dam in my throat.

"Didn't you have something special? A stuffed animal?" He's recalling our son with his cuddly Mickey Mouse, and how we always tucked his toy into a seat at the kitchen table or next to him in the minivan. After all these years, my husband still has the blanket and the Mickey, both kept safe on his closet shelf.

No stuffed animals. No dolls. Though I'm sure I must have had a doll. But after my mother was taken away in the ambulance, after lunch at the neighbor's, after an uncle gathered up me and my younger brothers and sister, I don't remember what happened next except for that days afterward, I was with nothing: not a hairbrush, not a comb, not a toothbrush, not a change of clothes—some of what was in the apartment would come later, when we knew we weren't going to return. My Pop must have packed up the two-bedroom apartment in the Bronx by himself. When I left the apartment without my mother that day, everything else was left behind too.

"I don't think it matters now, does it? It's been such a long time since I was four and a half."

My husband takes my hand. "I just don't believe it. You should have told me before."

"Why? What would you have done?" I'm hoping he doesn't say buy me a blanket or stuffed animal or doll.

"We've been married thirty years—"

"Thirty-three." I clear my throat, needing a glass of water.

He squeezes my hand.

"I'm thirsty," I say.

"Let's just sit here a moment together."

"I'm thirsty," I repeat, and I leave the room, and the house, into the muggy summer night.

Are You Still There?

I'm calling her, both of us hating the telephone. She uses the phone with the cord that winds around the kitchen into the hall and the pink and green bathroom. She hides there, the house's only bathroom. She could be interrupted at any moment by a younger sibling, or by her Pop, even though everyone else in the house is in bed. Still, she doesn't want to talk. She hasn't figured things out yet—*no, everything is fine*, but it isn't, and she doesn't know how to say this yet. It's easier to just say that everything is okay with the bath towels bunched on the floor, and the blue toothpaste dotting the porcelain sink, and the window open, and the autumn leaves slick on the rotting sill, and the air crisp with Ivory soap and the first cold rain of winter. *Are you still there?* you ask your younger self. *Where else would I be?* She exhales, the phone roughing against her mouth, a refusal to continue this conversation, which later your younger self will deem dumb, a dumb dream. Her hair is a tangle on her substantial shoulders. She wears tattered tee shirts to bed; she will for years. She doesn't know that soon she will be gone from this house; she believes it will never end, being twelve, being thirteen. Before she is eighteen, she will go. You want to tell the younger version of you, on the edge of the lid of the toilet seat, elbows on bare knees, arms blotched with purpled welts, that you will go far, that you will never have to return, that your memory will have blank spaces, long pauses to heal. When you are old, like you are now, some memories will arise when least expected. Like a call in the night, this knowledge of your younger self will awaken you, and you will know it is not a dream. You will be able to talk then, even if you do not want to talk.

ACKNOWLEDGMENTS

Thank you to all the literary magazines and anthologies that have published stories in *Carry Her Home*. Versions of these stories appeared in and/or were honored by the following:

"The Understanding" - 100-word stories

"The Piggyback Ride" - Fredericksburg Literary and Art Review

"Jones Beach State Park" - Silver Birch Press

"Wings" - Vestal Review

"Inside the Bureaucracy of My Mind" - *District Lines* anthology published by Politics & Prose bookstore

"D. C. Mechanic" - Gargoyle

"The Critique Group" - *Abundant Grace* anthology

"Little Bear's Apgar Score," "Shelley and Harvey" and "Counting Backwards" in three different web series from Akashic Books

"Beheaded" - Fiction Southeast

"No Mercy" - finalist, 2016 F. Scott Fitzgerald Short Story Prize

"Buttons" - finalist, Bethesda Magazine 2018 Essay contest

"Sweetness" - first prize, in the anthology *The Way to My Heart*

"Gargoyles and Stars"- first prize, in the 2016 *Writer Magazine* short story competition

•

To The Inner Loop Writer's Residency at the Woodlawn & Pope-Leighey Houses in Alexandria, Virginia during the summer of 2017, thank you. This week inspired me to write "O, Tomato," and "Buttons," the latter being the one story I call creative nonfiction to honor the near-forgotten memory of John known as "Button" and Elizabeth Montgomery Sharpe.

With great gratitude, thank you to the Arts and Humanities Council of Montgomery County (Maryland) for awarding me a FY18 Artists and Scholars Project Grant and for its support of the arts in our community.

With even greater gratitude, thank you to the passionate team at the Washington Writers' Publishing House headed by Kathleen Wheaton. Thank you, Jacob Weber, Robert Williams, Patricia Schultheis, David Ebenbach, and Barbara Shaw.

•

When I moved to the DC area five years ago, I found myself in two remarkable writing groups, both of which formed out of classes at the Writer's Center in Bethesda. Mohini Malhotra, Roberta Beary, Arne Paulson, Sheila Janega, Antonieta Romero, Alice Stephens, Danielle Stonehirsch, Therese Doucet, Jim McNeill, and Monica Hogan, thank you for every suggestion, every insight, every laugh and hug.

Kim Becker, Deborah Drennon, Elizabeth Kirkpatrick, Susan Kaplan, and Jessica Koenig, friends new and old, thank you.

•

To my husband Richard, and to my children Michael and Sara, and to my siblings Mark, Susan, and David, you make me who I am. Lastly, I send heavenward love to my parents, especially my Pop, who always teased that "Someday, Toots, you'll write a story or two about me." And of course, he was right.

BOOK CLUB DISCUSSION GUIDE

I have had the great privilege to be included in three books clubs (shout out to the ladies in Plainview-Old Bethpage, my first, and to the books clubs that welcomed me in Maryland). I hope these questions spark the same kind of smart, high-spirited conversations about *Carry Her Home*—and life—that my book clubs have shared.

1) Book clubs often focus on full-length works. How is the experience with short stories different for you?

2) Is there a story that particularly speaks to you? Why? Does reading flash fiction (stories generally under 1,000 words) feel different? How?

3) This collection contains many works of autobiographical fiction (the author even uses her parents' names and her name in some stories). How do you feel about this technique? Did it influence how you read the stories? Why do you think the author chose fiction over memoir?

4) Reflect on how the times have changed from the 1960s to today in terms of marriage, particularly intermarriage between people of different faiths, or ethnicities, or race?

5) What is typical about Murray and Louise's courtship and marriage? What makes it atypical? Do you think that they truly love one another when they decide to marry? What about later in their lives—does love stay true?

6) Pop, Matthew, and even, Caroline, are in the role of caregiver in several stories. How is the role of caregiver imagined in these stories? Do you agree or disagree with the character's actions or choices as a caregiver? Reflect on caregiver moments in your own life.

7) Louise's aneurysm is a defining event in the life of her husband and her children. How do some of the stories depict this event and its aftermath? Reflect on an unexpected life event, which changed everything for you and those near to you.

8) *Carry Her Home* opens with the father leaving in "The Understanding." The penultimate story is "What I Didn't Carry With Me," which ends with a wife/grown daughter leaving. Why is this important? What larger themes/ideas does this convey?

9) The last story in the collection, "Are You Still There?" has one character on the phone to another. Who are the two characters? Why do you think the author ended the collection with this story? If you could tell your younger self something, what would it be?

10) What does *Carry Her Home*, carry home for you?